SOME CAREERS ARE NOISIER THAN OTHERS

STRANGE STORIES BY
LYNDA FAYLE GILMARTIN

COVER ILLUSTRATIONS BY
MARCELO DA SILVA CASAQUEVIT

FAYLEBOOKS
DALLAS/FORT WORTH

ISBN: 0692057315.
ISBN-13: 978-0692057315.

DEDICATION

To the loving memory of
Robert Glen Gilmartin
and our granddaughter,
Meghan Elizabeth Gilmartin.

TABLE OF CONTENTS

ACKNOWLEDGMENTS

I wish to recognize my *teachers*, ranging from Marie Graves (who posted my early stories, on what she called "Lynda Fayle Day", throughout Polytechnic High School in Fort Worth) to Dr. Richard Tuerk at Texas A&M University-Commerce; the great *authors* Ray Bradbury, Eudora Welty and Benjamin Capps, for their influence on, and encouragement of, my literary efforts; my *former agent*, Don Congdon, at the Harold Matson Literary Agency; this book's *artist,* Marcelo da Silva Casaquevit, who brought my quirky concept to life in a wonderful cover; and Shelly Gerard and Jessica Akers, for *production services*. I am also eternally grateful for the love and support of my *family*, including - but not limited to - my *parents*, Esther Denham Fayle and Raymond Fayle; my *brother*, Raymond Fayle, Jr.; our *sisters*, Nancy Templeton and Bettie Taylor; my *children*, Eric (my colleague, proofreader and researcher on this project), Christian, Ingrid and Jacob; Dawn, my *granddaughter's mother*; and my *daughter-in-law,* Ashton.

SOME CAREERS ARE
NOISIER THAN OTHERS

EDITED AND PREPARED BY
ERIC GILMARTIN

1 SOME CAREERS ARE
<u>NOISIER THAN OTHERS</u>*

"I wonder who's being murdered now?" she said as she lay listening to the incessant tap, tap, tapping from the other room. She was stretched along a velvet sofa in the den, a cold towel pressed against her eyes. She felt as if some perverse woodpecker were lunching on her brain, rat-a-tat-tat, drilling ever inward, nearer and nearer to that soft vulnerable spot deep in her head which would explode at any moment with pain and anger. "And with what sort of weapon?" she whispered hoarsely. "A pistol? Butcher knife? Silk scarf?"

She threw the towel from her eyes and sat up, groaning. "No, nothing that ordinary, of course," she grumbled with a short sardonic burst of laughter. "A discreet pinch of an exotic poison, or an ivory-handled Oriental letter opener. Or poisoned stamps, perhaps. Hah, that would be good for the man of much correspondence."

She walked wearily down the hall and stopped at an open door, looking into the cluttered room where her husband sat, hunched over an ancient desk, his shoulders heaving in time with the jagged frantic rhythm of the typewriter.

The room smelled of stale smoke and dust and old books.

"Robert, it's almost six o'clock," she said, addressing the back of his worn tweed jacket. "Won't you stop for a moment and have a cocktail with me?" Her voice was sad, imploring.

The clicking keys tapped out the remnant of a sentence before he wheeled around in his swivel chair and looked up at her with a gleeful, childish grin. "Oh, darling, no, I can't. Carrigan's just got on to something," he said excitedly, "a most delectable clue. I mustn't let it get away. You do understand, sweetheart?"

"Carrigan, Carrigan, *Carrigan*!" she cried from the doorway in a voice straining with anger and contempt. "Why don't you ever murder *him* off? I'll gladly do it for you if you're too squeamish to put a dagger through the heart of that beastly detective. Why should *he* go scot-free time and time again in your morbid little world of mayhem?"

Her husband jumped from his chair and turned to her with a white face, staring at her as if she had indeed just committed murder. "My God, Margaret, how can you say such a thing?" He sighed, in a long exhalation of astonishment. "Why, you should be grateful to Carrigan, and to my 'morbid little world of mayhem,' as you put it. They, and an eager public, have given us everything – this house on the side of a cliff that you dreamed of all those years," he said in a rising voice, sweeping an arm around in a broad circle to indicate the house and the cliff and the angry blue ocean below, "and the cars and furs and servants,

12

and - yes, even your magically replenishing cabinet of gin."

She sucked in her breath and the rims of her pale-yellow eyes turned suddenly moist.

"Oh, darling, I'm sorry," he murmured, tilting his head to one side in an attitude of repentance. He did a little gliding dance to where she stood and placed one hand gently on her shoulder. "Why don't you run along now and fix the drinks and I'll be there shortly," he said, beaming his best coaxing smile down on her haggard, unforgiving face...

Tap, tap, tap. Clickety, clickety, clack. At midnight the sound seemed to come from very far away, distilled through the foggy, gin-soaked atmosphere of the porch. He had never come for the drink, of course, or for dinner. At eight she had taken him a plate of sandwiches and potato chips, which he acknowledged with a grunt, not realizing how long she stood behind him staring blankly at his rumpled head as it bobbed up and down with the outpouring of words he wrote.

She leaned back in the quilted chaise lounge, gripping her tall glass tightly with both hands and taking a noisy little sip, each time a gust of frigid air blew up from the shore and shuddered through her thin gown.

"It's the typewriter," she muttered drunkenly. "It's that infernal typewriter, with its tap, tap, tapping day and night. It's trying to kill me," she whimpered, and

13

her upper body began to shake. "That typewriter wants me dead."

Suddenly she sat upright as if the house had been jolted by a subterranean tremor. She looked out past the dark cliffs at a half-moon patch of moonlight on the water, listening for a sound – rather, for the absence of a sound.

"In which case I shall have to murder it first, won't I?" she whispered, letting the glass slip from her hand and land with a crash.

A gull dipped gracefully into a foaming whitecap below, shrieking as if in reply.

She found her way into the room with difficulty, not only because she was unsteady on her feet but because she didn't want to switch on any of the lights along the way. He would be in bed now, but perhaps not asleep – perhaps just lying in the dark contriving still more murders, more clues, more Sherlockian tracking and backtracking for his precious Carrigan.

She knew immediately when she had opened onto the right room, the *writing* room, by the thick and musty odor that pervaded it. She felt her way along the book-lined wall, stepping through wads of crumpled paper on the floor, until she reached the desk. She clicked on the tiny reading lamp and turned it upward. And, ah, yes, there it sat, her nemesis, the typewriter, quiet now but poised and ready for the morning's resumption of criminal activities.

And there was the sheet of white paper rolled just a short way up along the platen, for her husband always liked to end each evening's work by writing the first line of a new page. In this way, he maintained, he had no excuse for not barging right into work in the morning.

She rolled the sheet up farther and bent over to read it. "...just so happens that the bloody footprint was a size 10B, Mr. Waverly," it said. She felt a rage building in her breast until she thought she would burst.

"Bloody footprint, indeed," she whispered, and reached for the machine. She worked as silently as possible, bending and twisting the keys, terrified of creating noises that might be heard upstairs.

She slept restlessly that night, dreaming of a long corridor marked by a trail of size 10B footprints leading to a large echoing hall of clicking typewriters with animated, grinning faces. When she awoke the room was damp with morning fog, and a harsh sun glared through the open windows. She could feel it with her eyes closed; it seemed to burn right through her lids and to a tiny pinpoint of pressure deep inside her head. It throbbed there painfully, pulsing up and down, boom, boom, boom, rat-a-tat-tat, tap, tap, tap.

Tap, tap, tap! She jumped from the bed

15

and, pulling a satin robe about her shoulders, raced downstairs to her husband's work room.

She stood panting in the doorway, staring at him, dumbfounded, as he sat hunched over the typewriter as usual, working out the denouement of poor Mr. Waverly's misdeed.

"Good morning, Margaret," he said, without turning to look at her. "Did you sleep well?"

"I'm - I'm surprised to see you working so early, Robert," she stammered.

"Yes, I'm sure you are," he said in a voice as cold as the frosty cliffs. "Actually, I had some difficulty with the typewriter this morning. I found it lying on the floor with several of the keys bent. The result of a minor tremor during the night, no doubt. As a matter of fact, I seem to recall having heard a slight crashing noise just after I fell asleep last evening."

He swung around to face her with a smile - not his usual smile but one with a hint of darkness in it. "But I managed to straighten the keys and all's as good as new, except that the Q is sticking a bit. But then I've never been much of a Q-word man, myself."

"Oh, but I should think you *would* be, in your genre," she said, trying to make her voice sound light and playful. "After all, don't you have quite a few queer and quizzical people running about in a quandary?"

16

"Very amusing, Margaret, but now I really must get back to work." He gave a little push with his foot which sent his chair turning away from her.

"Oh, and by the way, I believe this belongs to you," he said, handing her a piece of paper which she grasped reluctantly with her fingers.

Across the top were the familiar words: "...just so happens that the bloody footprint was a size 10B, Mr. Waverly." But in the center of the page were the added words: DON'T EVER DO THAT AGAIN!

She was in more of a fever than ever that day. He was on to her for sure, and now he would never cease his typing. And she could not escape it anywhere, not in the patio, or the garden, or in the den, where she sat morosely at the bar for hours trying to drown the sound of it in her own mini-ocean of gin. Once, around dinnertime, she made a feeble effort at luring him away from the ghastly machine, which seemed to have attached itself to him like a permanent appendage.

"Cook's made a marvelous spread on the patio, dear," she offered with a tiny tingle of hope. "Wouldn't it be lovely to sit outdoors and listen to the surf for a while?"

"Oh, blast it, no, I can't, Margaret. Carrigan's being held hostage and I must think of a way to extricate him."

At that moment she felt her heart turn

to stone, a cold gray stone, and she knew that he would never penetrate it any more.

Once again that evening she sat in the chill night air, letting the brutal ocean wind embrace her like some vampire lover. But she had her bottle and her glass for comfort, and she took frequent, lingering sips which filled her with little warming fires. Tonight, she listened with a frozen determination, not to the surf or the screaming gulls, but for that delicious moment when the tap, tap, tapping would abruptly cease. When it came at last, she felt her ears roar with a thunderous silence.

This time she found the work room more easily, spurred on by manic intent, and she had taken the initiative of bringing tools. She switched on the reading lamp and found, as she expected, the clean white sheet of paper sitting like a virgin princess in the crown of the "royal" typewriter, marred only by the one lovely line along the top: "...touched by the sight of Delilah's lovely corpse."

"Oh, Delilah," she laughed, "I come to bury you," and she drew a heavy wrench from her pocket.

She couldn't sleep at all that night but tossed about the bed through an eternity of darkness, wrestling with the blankets and her conscience. Before dawn she rose and crept quietly to the hateful room to look once more on what she had done. The light was burning, though the room was empty, and — somehow! — the typewriter was intact, repaired, as though she had never maimed it.

"Surprised, my dear?"

She spun around to see her husband standing just behind her, grim-faced and bleary-eyed.

"I couldn't sleep last night for fear you'd try your nasty trick again, so I came down around three to find that indeed you had. I've repaired it once again, though, God knows, it will probably never be the same again."

"Robert, I —"

"You needn't say anything, Margaret. I know how troubled you are, how *sick*." He spoke the last word as if it were a foul-tasting morsel which he was spitting out.

Then he extended a rigid arm to her, holding a familiar sheet of paper in his hand. "We both seem to have a way with words these days, don't we?" He let the paper float to the floor and brushed roughly past her to his desk.

Bending down to pick it up, her heart pounded so fiercely that she feared it would fall out of her chest and land with a thud on the hardwood floor. Yes, it was the one-line paean to Delilah's corpse, but again there was an added message in the center of the page: THE COURSE YOU HAVE CHOSEN IS DANGEROUS. BEWARE!

She could hardly think any more, she could hardly breathe. Was he trying to drive her mad? Was she already mad?

She left the house immediately, taking a hastily gathered kit of booze and blankets down to the beach below, where she lay all day beneath an overcast sun, feeling her skin slowly scorching until it was pink and tender all over. But she didn't care. For the sound of his tap, tap, tapping drifted down from the window above, mingling with and overpowering the gentle rippling of the outgoing tide. How she wished for a raging surf right now, a furious tempest to wash away the hideous clacking of his mad, anthropomorphic machine.

At dusk he descended to the beach and stood looking down at her on the sand, a clenched fist planted firmly on each hip.

"Well, I see you've settled in for the day, my dear, you and your faithful friend," he said, pointing to the half-empty bottle of gin at her side. "And so, I shall be off to town for supplies. You won't be missing me much, I daresay."

"I hope you're taking bloody Cardigan along," she screeched as she watched him slouching off through the sand. "God only knows what sort of mess he'll get himself into without you!"

He threw a backward glance at her as he trudged with difficulty to the rickety wooden steps that ascended to the house, and in his eyes, showed the dull ugly look of a final and irrevocable disparagement.

She lay back on the gritty blanket and began to weep, painful wracking sobs shaking

20

the length of her too-thin, sunburned body. "Oh, murder, murder," she moaned. "Why doesn't he get it over with? Why doesn't he just dispense with me as quickly and as mercifully as the hordes of dime-store characters in all those horrid books he writes?"

She sat up with a jerk and began to wipe the grit and salty wetness from her face. "*He* writes! *He* writes! Sometimes I think that monstrous typewriter is the real brain and he is merely the tool, merely the fingers, arms and back that do the manual labor, the master's bidding. Well, we'll see who will murder who."

She struggled to her knees, then her feet, and stumbled forward in a zigzag toward the steps.

Halfway down the hall in the house she stopped, threw back her head, and flung both arms to heaven. "Just listen to it, will you? Just listen! No clicking, no tapping." She stood poised this way for a moment, then threw both arms exuberantly around her shoulders. "A perfect miracle of silence!" she cried.

The typewriter proved to be heavier than she had expected, perhaps because she was weak and strung out from too much sun and liquor. She tried lifting just the front of it, then let it drop with a bang to the desk. She sank into her husband's chair and gasped for breath, gazing at the sheet of paper on which he had been working when he left. "You should know you couldn't get away with it," it read. "Crimes of passion always have a way of turning back on the perpetrator."

"What drivel," she muttered and pushed herself up from the chair to have another go at her task. This time she heaved her body upward, with a great breath and hoisted the typewriter from the table with a tremendous strain of effort, letting it rest against her chest. In this way she staggered down the hall, the white sheet of paper flapping against her face.

She shoved front-ways through the double doors to the upstairs patio, barely able to breathe, and slid her feet along the wooden floor until she reached the railing. She rested the heavy machine on the railing's edge for a moment — without letting go of it and looked downward, dizzily. It was at least a forty-foot drop to the rocky beach below.

"Ah, Carrigan, dear friend," she sighed, "let us see you solve this one, you devil detective."

She took in a few quick breaths, then lifted the machine, and, twisting her body in a half circle, flung it outward across the rail. But her hands would not release, and the weight of the typewriter took her with it, crashing through the railing to the rocky depths below.

When her husband arrived home the next morning - having spent the night in a hotel — he found the yard filled with police cars and a great flurry of activity which seemed to lead down to the beach behind the house. Several officers were standing over her body, gesturing and conjecturing among themselves. She lay on her back, the typewriter sitting upright on her chest, unharmed, as though she had taken it to rest with her, for her fingers still clutched its sides, the knuckles still white with pressure.

He squatted down beside her, studying her pale and bloodless face. Even the rough sunburned skin along the brow seemed to have lost its color - it was as faded as the sun-bleached, pebbly rocks on which she lay. The raw wind off the ocean snapped at the paper in the typewriter, blowing it back and forth, giddily, like a small flag waving over her breathless body. He took the corners of it in his hands and held it still.

"Crimes of passion always have a way of turning back on the perpetrator," he read aloud, unconsciously savoring the last line of dialogue he had written. He began to roll the carriage up, in order to take out the paper, and suddenly his eyes grew wide and full of wonder. For there, in the center of the page, was the simple, enigmatic message: I WARNED YOU!

*Originally published as 'CRIME OF PASSION' in the November 1975 issue of *Ellery Queen's Mystery Magazine*.

2 THE LONG DREAM OF LUCY DASH

In the beginning it was difficult to tell that something was going wrong with Lucy Dash. It was only in retrospect that one had insight into certain aberrations in her behavior. Incidents which seemed trivial at the time, bore looming significance later, at least to those friends and neighbors bent on playing parlor psychiatry.

For a long while, it was simply a matter of forgetfulness; she forgot to pay the bills, she forgot appointments, she forgot to pick up certain necessities of modern life at the grocery store. One morning, as he dressed for work, she even forgot her husband's name and was reduced to getting his attention by saying, "Hey," several times and rather pointedly in his direction.

None of this seemed too peculiar, however, as Lucy's mental makeup had always been characterized by a certain lack of preciseness, a trait which had grieved her husband for many years and which he had endeavored to overcome through strenuous training.

The first inkling she had that her lapses of memory were straying beyond the ordinary came on a day when she forgot to collect the children from school; that is, she totally forgot their existence for one whole afternoon. It was as if she had never known them — they had not come to life in her belly and she had not spent many patient years tending to their growth and happiness. They simply did not exist for her that day. She was sitting staring blankly at the television set, not really listening to or watching the program, when a telephone call from a disgruntled teacher brought them back into her consciousness.

It was on that occasion that something deep inside her began to stir uneasily. Still, no one really noticed anything wrong with her in those days. She still laughed a lot and talked little. When they dined out with friends, she still picked nervously at her food and hummed along with the Muzak, until her husband pinched her under the table. She still had a slightly dreamy and unfocused look in her eyes and she still declined graciously to take sides in any heated discussions, all of which was normal and accepted without question.

It *was* true that she had had several minor accidents at home of late. She tripped over the vacuum cleaner in the living room and sprained her ankle, and one evening, while preparing dinner, she stuck her forefinger instead of a strip of peeled potato into a pot of boiling grease.

But she remained, to all outward appearances, a happy, busy mother and the proud wife of a young man on his way up. Friends talking to her on the phone couldn't know the pained expression she wore on the other end of the line while the receiver dangled from her hand, as if it hurt her to hold it.

The only signal of something going awry which might have been observed from the outside was her husband's increased irritability with her lack of presence of mind. One Sunday afternoon he came to the front door and called Lucy and the children into the driveway to witness the polish he had just applied to his car.

It was an ancient Mercedes-Benz which he had picked up at a bargain and rehabilitated and he was extremely proud of it. The other members of the family were not permitted to ride in it, of course, but they were expected to *look* at it a great deal, especially when he polished it, as he had just done this Sunday. It was something of a family ritual, trekking outdoors to see the shine on Daddy's car.

"Just look at it, just look at it," he said, making a circle around the car, moving as slowly and gracefully as a tiger. "Now *that's* a shine, *that* took some elbow grease, I'll tell you. Why, you can see your face in it." He bent over from the waist and peered at his grinning reflection in the gleaming metal, the chamois cloth still dangling from his hip pocket.

Then suddenly he straightened up and scowled at them. "But whatever you do, for God's sake, don't touch it. You hear me, you children, I don't want your grimy fingerprints all over my hard-earned polish job." And he continued to stare at them, reproachfully.

26

The children, who were bored, nodded their assent. They were missing the last half of a TV cartoon they had only seen twice before, and they were eager to be released.

"You see, children, this is what you can do when you really take pride in something," he said more softly, smiling again at last. He took the chamois from his pocket and rubbed it in little circles on the hood. "But the slightest touch will smudge it, will ruin its perfection."

Lucy walked over to the car. "You mean, like this?" she asked, rubbing her open palm across the shining fender.

"Stop! Stop!" he screamed, his cheeks flaming red with anger. "You've ruined it, you idiot!"

He did not speak to her the rest of that day. She could not even remember having done it herself. And it was just this sort of thing which was beginning to happen so often now. The very next day, for instance, while gathering the children into the car in a rush to get them to school, she slammed the door shut on the youngest child's thumb. Later, struggling with her memory in a fit of remorse and guilt, she could not remember having wrenched her body backwards from the front seat and having grasped the door handle to pull it shut. She only remembered the child's screams and the accusatory clamor of the other children. So many of her actual physical acts were becoming lost to her, as though her mind were taking leave of

27

her body more and more frequently. She found things done that she could not recall doing, and a little tingle of alarm began growing in her mind and in her breast. But she resisted it courageously, laughing when she felt like crying and offering impromptu explanations when she was totally in the dark. She even spoke to her husband one night of her increasing absentmindedness, to which he replied disparagingly that she had not enough to do with her time.

She accepted the wisdom of his remark and went next day to the library with the idea of checking out some books on macramé, and needlepoint.

She was standing staring at a row of books, not knowing what she was looking for or where she should have been if she *had* known, when she began to hear a woman sobbing.

My God, she thought, even in a *library*. There is no sanctuary from trouble, is there?

The sobbing became louder and louder, punctuated by prolonged and anguished moans, until it had destroyed her composure completely. It seemed to be coming from behind her, and whoever it was, was obviously desperately distraught. Why, she wondered frantically, don't they do something? A library is not the place. Good Lord, why don't they do something? She looked up and down the aisle to see if others were reacting as she was to this gross phenomenon. There were only two people within her vision, a tall woman with horn-rimmed glasses who was gazing serenely into a heavy, dark green volume, and a small boy at her side. He had a paper bag full of jelly beans which he was sticking onto the backs of the books on the shelves. He licked them first, then pressed them hard against the dusty jackets until they adhered. The finished product was not altogether unaffecting, thought Lucy, offhand.

Just then, the desperate woman behind them breathed a deep, agonizing sigh, as though she were dying painfully, and Lucy and the young boy looked at one another, caught each other's gaze in amazement.

He hears it, she thought, bewildered. *He* hears it, why don't the others? But then he almost instantly returned to his task of planting jelly beans on the books, casting one suspicious glance at her out of the corner of his eye.

The woman's sobbing reached a crescendo of painful intensity, until Lucy thought her eardrums would burst from it. She ran around the corner of the aisle and looked up and down for this poor, misbegotten creature who was being allowed to cry her heart out in the public library. She saw only two elderly men who were sitting at a table, peering into each other's faces and whispering. But the woman's crying grew still louder and louder; it seemed wrenched from the very bottom of her soul.

Lucy was on the verge of crying herself when she was approached by a stout young woman with a pencil perched precariously behind her ear.

"Can I help you find something?" she said in a voice wrought with distrust. "The indexes are in the front of the library, of course, but if you don't know how to use them, I'll be glad to help you find what you're looking for." She stuck the point of her pencil into her mouth and looked at Lucy with contempt.

"Yes, yes, *you can* help me find something," said Lucy, almost hysterically. She was still searching with her eyes for the source of the anguished voice which seemed so near. But just at that moment, the sobbing ceased, and she was suddenly aware of the quiet and serenity of the surroundings. One old man leaned across the table and tapped the other's arm with his finger to make a point. And there was nothing else to be heard anywhere, except for the slight rustling sound of the woman on the other aisle replacing her book.

She went home (without checking out a book), took two aspirins for no reason and retired to her bed. She fell asleep almost instantly, with the mindless ease of a person worn out from grueling labor. For most of the afternoon she slept, flitting in and out of restless dreams, but mostly sunk deep in a heavy blanket of oblivion. At one point, she dreamed that she saw herself sleeping on the bed and she knew in a strange way that she was dreaming. It was as if one part of her were awake and could speak to the other, sleeping part, could say, "Move now. Get up! Get up before it's too late."

In her dream she tried to move her arm, could not move her hand nor even flex her fingers, no matter how urgently she willed it with the conscious part of her mind. She was paralyzed.

This is silly, she thought in the dream. This is silly, it's only a dream and I can move if I want to, I can wake up. But she couldn't, not with any amount of struggling, and soon the conscious part of her dissolved into the dream.

When she awoke and sat on the edge of the bed, her head ached, and her body felt as if it had been weighted down with lead. But the memory of the woman sobbing in the library had become remote, had already receded to some innocuous corner of her mind where it held no importance. It was the dream of dreaming which disturbed her now. The recollection of her powerlessness over herself seemed vaguely ominous and threatening, and it haunted her all the rest of that day. She put off going to bed that night, for fear of having a recurrence of the paralyzing dream, until her husband came and gruffly coaxed her into the bedroom and made love to her in the usual manner. If he noticed anything strange in her attitude, he didn't mention it.

In the following days, she tried to fling off the eerie spell of her recent experiences in a flurry of contrived activity. She signed up for a class in needlepoint at a local fabric shop, though she hated the kind of slow, stilting labor it required, and she bought a large, expensive book on gourmet cooking. Between the two endeavors, she exhausted her consciousness, or tried to. The long afternoons she spent, standing at the sink, weeping over chopped onions and fumbling with the bits and pieces of unknown vegetables, in the effort to produce something akin to the tempting illustrations in the book. And in the evenings, she worried with the tedious threads and needles, chattering at her husband and children during the television commercials about the wonderful things she would make for them as soon as her skill was perfected.

But despite of it all, she could hardly deny anymore that something was going terribly wrong with herself, terribly, terribly wrong. It became an increasingly dreadful prospect to go to bed at night, yet she could hardly rouse herself in the mornings. And soon after lunch each day, a heavy, drugged sensation would begin creeping through her limbs and into her mind and she would be drawn to the awful bed once more, silently resisting and pleading, as if a spell had been cast over her, as if a demon or magician were leading her irrevocably into some forbidden world. And she had only to lay herself down for a moment to find that she was being offered up once more, like a sacrificial victim, to a world of fantastic dreams. Some were lovely, were like transparent sea shells, pale pink and orange and very luminous, and she floated through them in a transport of ecstasy, through light and airy rooms and marbled gardens, down cobble-stoned streets where all her heart's desires seemed to be rushing headlong to greet her. But most of them were awesome and terrifying, were built of the bits and pieces of a lifetime of fears.

She swooned on the airless heights of mountains; she drowned in dark and fathomless pools; she hurtled weightless into the black void of a starless and incomprehensible space. And worst of all, she was a prisoner — a miserable prisoner — of her dreams and of some ancient and befouling curse within herself.

Though she strived, with an almost deranged exaggeration, to strike a note of normalcy and stability in her waking life, she found it more and more difficult to shed the phantoms of her sleep, go about the business of the day. The dreams kept intruding, like fretful, spoiled little children demanding of her attention. Sometimes she could hardly grasp whether she was awake or sleeping, reality very nearly blending with the dreams, becoming an indistinguishable, twilight blur.

She awoke late one afternoon to find her husband and children staring down at her on the bed. The children looked perplexed; her husband, William, wore a familiar frown. "My God, Lucy, do you know what time it is?" he said, tapping on the crystal of his watch for emphasis. "I thought I told you this morning that I have a business meeting tonight and wanted dinner early."

She looked up at him through a dream-shrouded mist and extended her arms. "Oh, Daddy, can I please sit on your lap?" she said in a little girl's voice.

He slapped her smartly on the face and pushed her back against the pillow.

"Lucy, what on earth has gotten into you? What a way to behave in front of the children."

It was about two weeks after the incident with the car, just long enough for her husband to have forgiven her for it, when they all sat down to a nice Sunday dinner, the children wearing cute little plastic bibs from a lodge in New England where they had vacationed once. Lucy felt a familiar tingle of creepy uneasiness working in her breast, and she fidgeted in her chair. She had learned to be wary of such feelings lately, no matter *what* her objectivity told her about them. Suddenly she remembered the dreams and the sobbing woman and a whole phantasmagoria of monsters which had inhabited her consciousness, awake and sleeping, until she felt she would have to rise, and run screaming from the room. With her head bowed, she heard her husband's droning voice saying grace over a flock of beautifully glazed Rock Cornish hens on the table, and just as he finished, she said something terribly obscene, out loud. He looked up at her with bulging eyes and banged his fist down hard on the table, knocking over the gravy bowl and causing the brown liquid to run in turgid little rivers over the white tablecloth. The children stared at her in disbelief an instant before they dissolved into uncertain giggling. After a moment's hesitation, Lucy quietly pushed back in her chair, arose, and walked with dignity into the bedroom, where she lay down and once again put herself to sleep, without remorse or explanation.

Her husband sternly cautioned the children to pay no attention to what their mother had said and demanded that they eat their dinner, which they did as best they could, giggling and choking with bewilderment. He ate a portion of one of the birds, tearing the limbs from it angrily, and then he gathered up his golf clubs and walked through the front door without a word.

When he returned several hours later, he was amazed to find the table intact as it had been, cluttered and smeared, and the children running in and out through the glass door, dirty and disheveled. He stormed into the bedroom with the intention of lecturing Lucy about her negligence and laziness, but he found her still asleep, and something about her appearance stopped him as he was about to wake her. She was huddled in a tiny little bunch on one edge of the bed and her face looked pale and pinched.

Her brows were knit, and her clenched hands made involuntary movements toward her chin, as if she were trying to forestall something in her sleep. She looked as if she might have been having a bad dream, which she was.

In the dream, she was on a roller coaster, the devil's very own contraption, to her way of thinking. As a child, she had been forced to ride on one — some adult's idea of the proper way to instill courage in a child — and she had never been as terrified, either before or since. In her dream, the roller coaster car in which she rode, front and center, kept approaching that hideous, hairpin turn at which it seemed it would go flying out into space but which it always maneuvered, with a neck-breaking jerk, at the last possible moment. She felt the hopeless terror rising in her as the car approached the invincible turn and she heard herself scream. Then everything went blank and then she was approaching the turn again, over and over, with no prospect of release, no way to get off. Each time, she could feel in advance the nothingness of space beneath her and the terrible, dread sensation of falling.

Around midnight she woke up crying and wondered where she was. Her husband didn't stir beside her, but she could feel the warmth of his body and could hear his breathing, and it soothed her. She wasn't on a roller coaster, after all, and she wasn't about to drop down from some great height. She lay back on her pillow and began to breathe in deep, rasping sighs. It was one way of knowing she was still all right, it was a way of controlling things, to breathe this way.

Still she could not fling off the feeling of the dream, no matter how hard she tried to push it from her mind. And it was not so much the thought of the roller coaster ride which made her tremble underneath the blankets but an eerie, creeping sense that she had embarked upon a journey from which she would never return.

She lay shivering in a cold sweat, tormented by the feeling that she had turned a corner in her life, passed over a bridge into another, strange and awesome world, leaving her old life behind forever.

When it was nearly daylight, she drifted mercifully at last into a dreamless slumber, her cheeks still flushed and moist from the terrors of the night.

At seven, when William Dash came and sat on the edge of the bed with a steaming cup of coffee — a rare, conciliatory act — he found that he could not rouse his wife. Her lips were slightly parted, as though she had been stopped in the middle of a smile, and little tracks of dried tears ran like crossroads from the corners of her eyes down her pale temples. Her breathing, though even, was very faint, her pulse the merest ticking in her wrists and throat, almost as if she were barely inhabiting the still body anymore. Late that evening, when she still lay like a calm and motionless Sleeping Beauty, a doctor came and was ushered into the bedroom, become almost like a morgue now, while the curious, bewildered children were shushed and waved away. He pulled back the sheet and tapped at her knees with a rubber-tipped instrument. He touched her cool forehead repeatedly and held her lifeless wrists and wore a puzzled look on his face.

Once, during this ritual, she awoke enough to see her husband's face bent over hers and she could hear him speaking, indistinctly, as though they were separated by a dense cloud. "Lucy, this is ridiculous, you know. If you have any problem, you can come to me with it. Frankly, I didn't know you were this weak! Lucy? Lucy? This is ridiculous. This is costing money, you know?"

But the words were not at all clear to her. And besides, she was traveling very far away again, very, very far away to a garden, a lovely garden of such an intense and throbbing greenness that it was almost blinding to the sight. In the distance she saw what seemed to be a group of snowy, white clouds floating just above the ground. And suddenly she realized that they were not clouds but white-robed figures, hooded monks clothed all in white. They moved as gracefully as dancers, leaping about on the green-carpeted lawn of the garden, their white robes billowing and flowing in the gentle breeze stirred by their dance. And they were laughing and singing as they tossed a small, pink ball from one to another.

"Here, Lucy. Lucy, here, catch the ball," a voice called out to her, and she reached up her arms to the tiny, pink sphere whirling in an endless revolution through the amber sky. Down and down it came, faster and faster, through an eternity of breathless waiting, but what she caught and held, finally, was not a ball at all but the head of a dark-haired baby, with black and staring eyes, its rosy lips smiling sweetly up at her from her cupped hands.

The doctor mumbled something about "psychosomatic coma," and scribbled the name of a psychiatrist on a small, square pad.

"But how in God's name can a psychiatrist help a person who is in a coma?" asked Lucy's husband irritably.

"Well, that is very difficult to say," replied the doctor, shrugging his shoulders into his overcoat. "Only time will tell, only time will tell."

The children were thereafter forbidden to enter the room in which their mother lay entombed in her mysterious, consuming sleep. After a while, with the benign and protective memories of youth, they very nearly forgot its existence, as though it had been boarded up, like an attic full of useless relics. They played through the house as carefree as ever, a gray-haired nanny to care for them now, and when they passed by the door which was never opened anymore, perhaps they glanced at it, wonderingly, a moment and moved on.

William Dash had moved all his belongings into the spare room across the hall from where his wife lay in stately slumber. Each night before retiring, he eased open the door of her room and gazed at the still, white figure on the bed, surrounded now by the strange and complex paraphernalia which kept her alive, the narrow tubes which ran like tributaries feeding life into her bloodstream, life-stream. And night after night, he repeated a ritual chant over the lifeless body on the bed, an incantation without which he could garner no rest from his perplexing torment.

"How could you do this to me, Lucy?" he would whisper in a solemn, temple voice. "What have I ever done but work and slave for you, to give you this beautiful house and all the comforts of life and three wonderful children for you to cherish and mold? Why have you done this to me, Lucy Amelia Dash?"

Lucy — though it seemed to those around her that she might as well be dead - was still alive and dreaming, and traveling, on the wings of Morpheus, through exotic jungles; endless, thirsty deserts; primeval swamps where long-tailed lizards crawled out from under rocks to gaze with their shiny, bead eyes upon the chill, uncompromising

40

light of earth's first day; to Jupiter and back; and to a myriad of other terrifying, enchanting destinations unimagined and unimaginable by those in the waking world.

In her last dream, she strolled through a gaudy circus midway, beautiful, grotesque faces staring out at her from every stall. A bearded lady, a tattooed man, a shriveled little monkey figure which was neither fish nor fowl who reached out a hairy hand to her through a pastel curtain as she passed. She extended her arm, touched the fingertips and recoiled.

She couldn't remember where she had been last, only that it had been a long time since she had been conscious of being anywhere at all. All around her was noise and lights and a kind of depraved gaiety she had never been privileged to witness before. A polka-dotted, red-nosed clown whom she had seen once on a poster as a little girl somersaulted past her, and she was conscious of the sweet and rancid odor of popcorn and that strange and otherworldly substance known as cotton candy. The sound of raucous laughter and of trumpets blaring "Lady of Spain" filled her ears until she felt she would burst from it all.

She wondered suddenly if she should go home, if she *could* go home, for she could not remember now where it was, or even if there was such a place.

With tears welling in her eyes, she wandered off into a grassy spot between the parking lot and the main tent of the circus, the noise of the midway only slightly diluted and distilled by the meager distance she had put behind her.

She sat down on the stump of a tree and buried her face in her hands.

"Well, now, I haven't seen a face like that since Cassandra urged Agamemnon not to take a bath." The voice which spoke to her had the tiny, tinkling sound of those little chimes which blow together in the wind. Lucy looked up to see a little man, dressed all in black, standing with one spat shoe crossed over the other as he leaned cockily upon a gold-tipped wand. "As I was saying, I haven't seen a visage that dire and dark since Caesar looked his old friend Brutus in the eye for the last time."

"Who are you," moaned Lucy, "and what do you want?"

"Generius Giles at your service, my lady, master magician of the ninth universe, and what, may I ask, could I do to cause those tears to disappear from your lovely cheeks?" He bowed deeply to her and, waving his hand, a little puff of smoke arose and dissolved, revealing a plump bouquet of blood-red roses on the ground before her feet.

"Oh, go away," she pleaded. "You cannot give me what I want. Not all the roses or rabbits in the world can give me what I want."

"But just ask and it is yours," insisted Generius Giles. "Is there some devil I might exorcise from your life? Is there some wish I can make come true?"

42

In her dream, through the last fading rays of her earthly existence, Lucy looked up at him and wondered if she might really ask him for the one thing she truly wanted.

"Yes, yes?" asked Generius Giles, grinning, as if he read her mind.

"What I would like," said Lucy, haltingly, in a quiet voice, "is for you to make the whole world disappear."

"The whole world?" he asked wonderingly. "The whole world?"

"Yes, the whole world," she said, firmly and resolutely.

"But madam, if I make the whole world disappear, then there will be no one left to bring it back, not even me."

"Yes, I know," Lucy said, smiling softly, "and that will be fine, just fine, thank you."

He hesitated a moment, looking wide-eyed and bewildered. Then, raising the wand, he gave a little flick of his hand and the long dream of Lucy Dash was over at last.

William Dash was relieved to have his wife's body removed from the house. Her life-in-death presence had become an embarrassment and, besides, the children were growing older now and they needed the space which she was taking up so irrelevantly. He turned the room into a den, with a maple desk and paneled walls and a book shelf which reached up to the ceiling. But he never spent much time there, after all, for whenever he settled into the leather-cushioned captain's chair, he had the vague notion that the room and its accouterments smelled of popcorn and greasepaint, and sometimes, late at night, he thought he heard a small, shrill sound, which might have been a mouse, but which sounded much more like a tiny, choking sob, or a laugh.

3 <u>THE MONKEY MACHINATION</u>

The drawn, hairy arm, which reached out to Alfred through the door, waving a jungle greeting, was not Betsy's. Not unless she had undergone a dramatic metamorphosis, during the day. Nor was it her voice erupting from the living room in a delirious, grunting squeal, like half a soundtrack from an old Tarzan movie.

"Good Lord!" cried Alfred, stumbling backward down the steps, away from the cloying, rubbery fingers which had touched his face.

Betsy flung open the door to reveal herself, standing, Madonna-like, upon the carpet, clutching a thing which seemed all wild, akimbo arms and legs which climbed up and over her and back around again.

Eyes bulging, Alfred was about to rush forward and attempt a rescue, when his wife cried out to him, "Oh, Alfred, isn't he *darling*?"

She ducked her head just in time to avoid a free-swinging, furry hand, then looked down at the dark lump at her breast, and purred, "Say hello, to Mr. Moto."

Alfred fell off the porch for sure then and was covered in an instant by the grinning, brown beast, which bounced up and down on his chest with its flat, thudding feet, all twelve of them, or so it seemed.

"Oh, Alfred, isn't that *cute*?" squealed Betsy, clamoring out in the yard to kneel beside them. "He's telling you he likes you. Oh, I know we're just going to be the *happiest* little family," she said, clasping her hands together fervently.

"A monkey?" said Alfred, slowly and deliberately. "A *monkey*, Betsy?"

He was staring morosely in his third martini, trying not to notice the coarse, brown hair on the lip of his glass.

"I would have brought you anything you wasted, a dog or a cat or even a cockatoo to talk to, but a *monkey*, Betsy?" he said in the same, slow, incredulous voice.

"Hey, Alfred, don't be difficult. You know how lonely I get with you gone all day. And even when you're here, you hardly ever talk to me, except to grunt an order for some food... or something *else*," she said, looking at him sideways through narrowed eyes, with her lips pursed in a reprimand.

There was a grunt from another quarter then, as Mr. Moto leapt into her lap and threw his ape's arms around her neck. They clung and swayed, the two of them, making strange, ungodly noises at each other as they rocked in their primitive embrace.

"And Mr. Moto can keep me company now. Won't you, darling?" she asked the creature in a soft, provoking voice.

Alfred stared at them, wondering if he had staggered, unawares, into a Fellini movie or a bad dream. Then he banged his fist down hard on the table.

"But, damn it, Betsy, how can a dumb, squeaking *monkey* keep you company?"

She looked up at him with the same, narrow-slit glance and spoke in her best schoolmarm tone, "Don't be silly, Alfred. Everybody knows that monkeys are practically human. Even better in some ways, because they're easily pleased and don't complain." She turned to the Capuchin with a sweet smile and cooed, "Aren't you almost just like a little man, Mr. Moto?"

The creature bared its teeth at her in a wide, mindless grin and, with a quick little leap, entwined its legs about her waist. Alfred gasped and poured a fourth martini.

"Fried bananas *again*?" he wailed, a few days later, pushing away his dessert plate.

"Well," said Betsy. "You know how quickly bananas spoil, and yet I must keep plenty on hand for Mr. Moto."

"If he's so god-damned human, why can't he learn to like chocolate mousse?"

"You're just being petulant, as usual," she said, picking up her knitting, a half-finished checkered sweater in a child's size. "Isn't he asking just like a naughty little boy, Mr. Moto?" she asked the monkey, who had jumped to the table to lick up Alfred's fried bananas.

Alfred subdued a sudden, violent impulse and cleared his throat.

"I'm...I'm going into the den to work on my report for Mr. Gunderson," he said, and waited for Betsy's customary objection that he never spent his evenings with her. But her clicking needles never missed a beat,

47

and she said, without looking up, "That's fine, dear. Mr. Moto and I are going out for a little walk in the park."

Alfred drifted to the den in a sort of daze, picking his way through some newly-acquired, jungle-motif debris: a wilting rubber plant, a nest of stubbly bamboo branches in a corner of the living room, a strangling web of netting draped across the archway in the hall. And at the entrance to the den, he tripped on a plastic bongo drum.

At midnight, when he hadn't written yet a single word for Mr. Gunderson, or even thought of him, he heard the front door click shut and Betsy's laughter. And the misplaced, tropical yelping of the monkey.

"...And did you see that couple on the beach," he heard her saying, "the way they jumped apart when we came down the sidewalk?"

She dissolved into a fit of giggling, accompanied by the monkey's coarse, atonal grunts. And at this point, Alfred had a searing mental picture of Mr. Moto's thrusting leap upon his wife.

After six years of bliss with Betsy, everything seemed turned upside down in his life, quite literally in some respects. The house was no longer the quiet, dilettante's retreat it had once been but a noisy, throbbing carnival of confusion, with tables upended and books scattered and bits of broken crockery on the kitchen floor. And

48

just when he least expected it – when he had for a moment, through some strenuous act of will, forgotten the monkey's existence – Mr. Moto would come bounding through the room or swinging from the chandelier to land, with a teasing and triumphant yell, upon his shoulders.

On such occasions, Alfred felt the full potential of his baser instincts. "Must you always have this... this *animal* at the table with us?" he growled at dinner, realizing the impotence of his complaint.

"Well, I don't see why not. He certainly has better manners than some *humans* I know," Betsy remarked pointedly. "At least he doesn't pick the crust from his chicken pie or build pyramids with his peas."

Mr. Moto smiled, stretching his pinkish, rubber lips across his mile-wide teeth, and flipped his fork into the air. It landed with a clink on Alfred's plate.

"You call *that* manners?" cried Alfred, dabbing at the gravy on his plate.

"That's just his way of telling you how childish you're behaving," said Betsy, and she reached across the table to pat at Mr. Moto's hairy chin with her linen napkin.

Alfred declined, rather severely, his portion of fried bananas and retired to bed, slipping on a cluster of discarded peanut shells along the way.

From the bedroom he could hear their mingled chattering and the monotonous droning of the TV set.

Occasionally, Betsy laughed or raised her voice in exclamation. "Oh, did you hear

49

that?" she sang out at one point. "David Letterman says that scientists who work with monkeys, give them *ape*-titude tests."

A fierce, thumping beat rolled through the house, and Alfred guessed that Mr. Moto liked the joke.

With something like a sob, the Capuchin turned and began to pound his pillow, until a single, white feather rose and fluttered in the air.

On Sunday, when they always drove to the country for fresh vegetables and fruit — really, just an excuse for an outing together and a breath of country air — Betsy dressed Mr. Moto in the checkered sweater she had knitted in record time.

"Now, don't you look just the perfect gentleman?" she asked rhetorically, patting his brown, burr head.

She took him by the hand, or rather, *paw*, and led him to the door, while Alfred stood by sulking, nervously jingling the car keys in his pocket.

"And like all gentlemen, you must open the door for a lady," she said in that peculiar, high-pitched voice she reserved for her comments to the monkey.

Then, wonder of wonders, the beast lurched forward and, with a frantic scuffling at the knob, pulled open the door and stood back for her to pass.

"*Thank* you, sir," said Betsy in her falsetto for the monkey, twisting backward to bow daintily as she exited.

In the car, Alfred smoked three pipefuls

and didn't say a word. Not that he needed to, for Betsy went on like a long-playing CD, nicked and sticking at some points, to be sure.

"And over here, Mr. Moto, is Stillman's Bridge, where forty Union soldiers waited seven days for orders from General Grant, which never came, of course, because he was drunk and didn't know they existed. Which is just like a Yankee. So not cognizant of other people's feelings," she said, and cleared her throat a little loudly.

Alfred slouched in the driver's seat and mentally disavowed New Jersey.

"And, look, over there," she continued, catching her breath, "is Denham Woods, where they found the dinosaur bones, I believe. Oh, you would love it there, Mr. Moto, so much wildlife just *waiting* to be preserved."

Mr. Moto jumped up and down in the back seat in his checkered sweater, emitting frequent, lusty squeaks, which seemed unrelated to the landmarks along the way.

Alfred could feel his moist, hot breath upon his neck as he drove, and he swerved the car wildly at times, whenever a shuddering repugnance overcame him. But mostly he puffed on his pipe and tried to think of ripe mangoes from Hawaii and white-kernel corn and crisp, leafy lettuce waiting down the road.

"And just ahead, Mr. Moto," Betsy began, doing a reverse half-nelson in her seat to see him, "is Pelham Point, where two lovers once leapt..."

"Oh, shut up!" blurted Alfred, swerving

51

crazily to miss a load of ripe tomatoes. He felt the sky fall on his head, with a heavy, thudding crunch, which was Mr. Moto's firm, adjudicating paw.

"*We* are not speaking to you," said Betsy that night, holding her besweatered monkey by the hand. Whereupon the two of them marched and gamboled, respectively, to the inner recesses of the house.

"And a banana mousse to you, too," shouted Alfred, seeing them off with a flippant wave of hand, bitterly. But seeing Betsy go, arm in arm with Mr. Moto, he felt something inside him draw taut, as if it would break and send him flying in pieces into outer space.

He sat on the patio until the murky thickness of encroaching dawn engulfed him.

"Oh, well, monkey see, monkey do," he muttered drunkenly at last, raising his glass before him like a shield to ward off demons. Then he struggled to remember if he had closed the bedroom door last Thursday night.

When there was barely an hour left before the necessary time of his departure for the city, he tiptoed into the bedroom and found Betsy shivering with sleep, frail and white beneath the covers. "Betsy?" he whispered, laying a gentle hand upon her arm. "Betsy, I've come to make amends," he said, smiling a fuzzy little smile.

He sank onto the bed beside her and took her frosty cliffs of shoulders in his hands.

"Oh, is that you?" she murmured, rolling

over with a long exhalation of drowsy breath.

"Yes, it is I, dearest," he moaned, bending to her parched lips.

Somewhere between idea and execution, "Fate" dropped down from the skylight, with a rending, guttural shriek, bounding upon the bed until it moved a foot across the floor.

Betsy sprang up and stared at her husband with glistening, gold-flecked eyes. "*Honestly*, Alfred," she rasped in a sleep-besotted voice, clutching at Mr. Moto and her black peignoir, "can't you let us get any rest?"

Something there is in the mind of man, which dies at such a question.

Alfred didn't eat or sleep well after that. Sometimes he lay alone in the vast bed, with thunder in his stomach, listening to Betsy's tinkling laugh and Mr. Moto's chirping from the other room. At other times, he rose later at night and wandered through the garden, looking at his hand as if to see how so much had slipped through his fingers, unawares.

His face took on the dark and cavernous look of the besieged, his fingers twitched, and his once fluid and aristocratic speech became a sort of harsh and trepid grunting.

Sitting in the chambered bedroom of *Gunderson and Johannsen* one afternoon, he looked down at the blurred and waiting figures in his lap, swallowing a yawn.

Then he gulped down another yawn and

flung his arm up and backward, to scratch at the nape of his neck. A small, honking sound escaped him, which was mistaken by one and all for a stifled cough.

"...and *now* hear from *Alfred* on the latest developments in his *Washee Wizard* project," Mr. Gunderson was saying in his flowing, roller coaster voice.

But Alfred continued digging a little hole in the back of his neck with two fingers, and honked yet again, through a great, gaping yawn.

"Alfred's *report*, I say, on the *Washee Wizard*..." repeated Mr. Gunderson, with an upward lilt.

"Uh, yah," said Alfred in a low grumble, snapping to. He bent forward and tried to make some sense of the melting butter in his lap. "Our latest cost analysis shows us that we stand to make approximately a 33% profit on the product. And *this*, gentlemen," he said in a strangled voice, while his ears popped, painfully, "is before the inevitable refinements in production."

A long sigh went through the room and many rows of kernelled teeth beamed their approval. "Yah? Yah?" said Mr. Gunderson. Then he slapped a fat hand to the table and roared, "Well, I'll be a monkey's uncle!"

Something cracked in Alfred's consciousness. "Well, *I* won't," he cried in a hoarse voice, snapping a pencil in two and stomping from the room. He went directly home, forsaking a dentist's appointment and a golf lesson. But standing on the front porch, before he dared to touch the knob, he did a fleeting survey of his own, incongruous situation.

He remembered all the jungle movies he had ever seen, where a tall, hairy-chested man beat on his breast before a simpering and compliant female. Then, clasping her roughly about the waist, or somewhere, they would swing off into midnight shadows of the forest depths. And all the monkeys and hyenas and assorted animal wildlife were merely bit players, adding their touch of raucous color to an otherwise monotonous and monochromatic backdrop. Me Tarzan, you Jane. Right? Right. Since when did *Cheetah* ride off into the sunset with the girl?

"Betsy, we must talk," said Alfred, kicking aside a braided bamboo mat in which his toe was caught.

"Hush, Alfred," she hissed. "Mr. Moto and I are watching a performance of 'The Hairy Ape' on public television."

The monkey cupped a broad, hairy hand to his flapping ear and shushed at Alfred through his simian teeth, sending Alfred fleeing to the kitchen before a wafting cloud of aromatic breath.

"Well, what did you want to talk about?" said Betsy when she came into the kitchen at last.

Before he could answer, however, she turned to the monkey and spoke in that intimate, oily tone that Alfred had always considered his very own, rare possession: "You must run along and dress for dinner, Mr. Moto. We're going to the Carsons', and they have the *darlingest* chimp named Daisy.

"But try not to make me too jealous," she laughed.

Mr. Moto rebounded from the sink to the floor to the breakfast counter and, in one long, graceful swoop across the living room by way of the chandelier, landed on all fours in the hallway.

"And why don't you wear that houndstooth vest I knitted?" Betsy called after him, to which Mr. Moto responded with a gleeful shriek. Then she turned back to Alfred. "And what can I do for *you*?" she asked, very much in the manner of a receptionist in an employment office.

"Betsy, sit down," he said firmly, in his lowest range. But just what he meant to say next escaped him somehow and he grasped frantically at a fading mental picture of Johnny Weissmuller standing tall and proud in a bulging loincloth. "I... uh... want to talk to you about this 'monkey business' that's been going on around here lately."

"Oh, Alfred, that's cute," she said, "but I really haven't time right now. We're due at the Carsons' in an hour."

"You'll *take* time," he growled, throwing up a limber arm to get an itching spot below his second rib. Scratching through layers of rayon and polyester, he could get no relief; he grimaced, exposing his capped and fluoridated teeth in a wide, maniacal smile. And then, that same, strange honking sound escaped him: "*Aarnk*," as though he were reaching for a popcorn sliver on his tonsil.

"Really, Alfred, it isn't nice of you to

ridicule Mr. Moto. And, anyway, you do a terrible imitation of a monkey. They're much more melodic than that."

After dinner at the Carsons', Daisy and Mr. Moto went out to gyre and gimble on the lawn, while their human masters crouched about a low table in the living room, sipping coffee.

"Yessir," said Harvey Carson, "there's nothing like a monkey to show us so-called human beings up for what we are. What's the difference, after all, in swinging from the limb of a tree and dangling from our own petards?" He laughed heartily. "Don't you think so, Al?"

Alfred dipped into the fruit bowl on the coffee table, picking out a golden, green-streaked banana. "Personally," he said, peeling the banana, strip by tender strip, "I think that monkeys are for the birds. Or whatever."

Betsy scooted to the edge of her seat and piped up in a sweet, mincing voice. "Actually, Alfred is awfully jealous of the attention I give our Capuchin. Why, he acts just like a pouty little boy, at times - as if there weren't enough cookies to go around." She gave him a sideward glance, and the soft, rounded corners of her Southern drawl straightened out into a hard line. "Of course, if he gave me half the respect that Mr. Moto does, he'd be surprised at my reaction." A sudden thunderous cleavage of the earth occurred then, which was Daisy and Mr. Moto adjourning from their play.

"Well, hello there, old girl," said

Harvey, reaching out to take his monkey in his arms. Daisy was smaller than Mr. Moto and dressed in a dotted-Swiss pinafore. She jumped up and down on Harvey's knees until his face took on a slight, purplish tinge.

"Oh, gracious Mr. Moto," trilled Betsy, bending over to straighten his vest and tie, "you had Mama just a teensy bit worried when you didn't come back for so long."

"*Aarnk, aarnk,*" sang Mr. Moto, melodically, and jumped into her lap.

"*Aarnk, aarnk,*" retorted Alfred, pawing at his second rib.

Driving home, he devised a second, desperate plan, which bore a striking resemblance to the first plan, enacted with conspicuous unsuccess a few days before. "Tomorrow's Sunday, you know?" he muttered, taking Betsy's arm as they crossed the threshold.

"We could sleep late? Have breakfast in bed? And maybe something besides breakfast? Um?" He blew on her cheek and felt his own hot breath turn back on him.

"Sorry, dear," said Betsy, "but I'm taking Mr. Moto to the Vet's first thing in the morning."

"What for?" screeched Alfred.

"Why, to have his heart and lungs and all examined, of course."

"But what about *my* heart?"

"Don't be absurd, Alfred. You're as healthy as an ox."

"Ox! Monkey! What *is* this, a zoo?"

"There you go again," she cried, "acting so pig-headed and stubborn..."

"Would you cut it out with the animal comparisons?" he wailed. "I've had it up to *here* with animals. I want to wallow in human beings, for a change. I want to go to Times Square at noon and roll around in an endless sea of upright, two-legged, hairless *Homo sapiens*, for Christ's sake."

"Well, that is just the silliest thing I ever heard, Alfred," said Betsy in her calming, Red Cross voice, "inasmuch as you're an animal yourself, which, God knows, is not strictly speaking."

Alfred experienced a brief anxiety that he would grind his teeth to a fine powder as he closed the garage door. Is this what an animal does? he wondered, startled by the volume of his inner voice. Does an animal do this? And does the animal create and put on the market a product, like *Washee Wizard*, which will wax your floors and six feet up your walls in half the normal time? And does an animal calculate and formulate and extrapolate and interpolate, till there is "*Pi*" in the sky?

Hell, no! his drunken and obstreperous inner voice proclaimed. An animal eats and sleeps and breathes, in blank oblivion. And plays... yes... and makes love without remorse... yes... and rolls in cool grass without a conscience. And knows no time... and answers to no voice... and... and just lives until it dies.

He stood in the coal-black shadow of the

towering trees a long time, looking up. I must trim that oak tree in the corner, he thought. Its branches bend too far, touch the street.

The hell you will! whispered his inner voice, a fierce, hissing echo in his brain.

"Alfred, you must come and see this with us," called Betsy from the living room, as he was turning the second bolt on the front door.

"Mr. Moto and I are watching *King Solomon's Mines*. The scenery is just too lush for words. And you would *love* the quaint native dancers."

Mr. Moto squawked and did a nosedive to the couch.

Something unbidden, or nearly unbidden, arose and thundered in Alfred's breast, like waves accosting a defenseless shore. His eyes glowed like steely marbles in the dimness of the night light in the hall. He approached Betsy from behind, with all the silence of a stalking animal, his moist, hot breath preceding him.

"Oh, those people have *so* much rhythm..." Betsy had started to say, when Alfred pounced on her, digging his whiskery chin into her neck.

He lifted her up and out of the vinyl recliner, groping backward with his load. "Alfred, what on *earth*...?" she squealed. Then she noticed the dark and predatory gleam in his eye, felt his sumptuous sigh along her cheek.

"Down, Mr. Moto, down," she shushed,

60

frantically waving away her monkey as he started up in protest, bounding across the couch to save her.

"Betsy, we're going to bed," growled Alfred, his voice rumbling up like some distant ground-swell of thudding hooves. And something in his sinuous grasp, and in the sudden of rain of moisture down his face, caused her to sink back with a sigh and bite her lip.

"Why, yes, of course, dear," she murmured, reaching up to push a damp lock from his forehead. "And we'll have croissants for breakfast."

"*Aarnk*?" asked Mr. Moto in bewilderment.

"*Aarnk*," declared Alfred, boldly flexing his fingers.

And then, entwined in one another like the twisting branches of a banana tree, Alfred and Betsy swung off to bed together, leaving Mr. Moto to watch the late show alone.

4 THE MAN WHO LOVED A HOLE*

"Actually, I'm only doing this for a lark," said Wilbur Barrington, drawing a printed silk handkerchief from his pocket, with which to wipe the shiny beads of perspiration blooming on his temples. "I thought it might be rather fun to have a pet for a while, something to break the monotony of people, you know." He laughed nervously, looking around him at the vast array of caged animals.

"Oh, well, we have the largest selection of exotic animals to be found anywhere around," said the little man, who looked something like a mutated animal himself. "Iguanas have been *very* popular the last couple of years, though they do have a tendency, to become very... well... *slumberous* in the winter months. And then you have the problem of disposing of them."

Wilbur made a grimace of delicate disgust, which inspired the little animal-man to go on. "And then, of course, you have your birds," he said, waving his hand toward a fantastic variety of colorful, caged birds whose simultaneous shrilling produced a deafening cacophony. Reading Wilbur's expression, he hastily added, "Of course, they're much too common for a man of your tastes." And he dismissed the birds with a flutter of soft, white fingers.

The pet-man looked intensely thoughtful for a moment, shining his beady little eyes on the corrugated ceiling while he made a low whistling sound through his teeth. "But, ah, I have it," he said, drawing the words out with obvious relish. "We *do* have something here that might be just to your liking, inasmuch as you are obviously a man of great breeding and distinction, in such matters. We have been privileged to receive recently, a shipment – limited, you understand, oh, very limited – of the rarest and most elite domesticable pet to be found anywhere on earth."

He spoke in a whisper of vulgar intimacy. "As a matter of fact, I really shouldn't even be speaking to you of this, except that it's apparent to me that you're the sort of man who can appreciate what I am about to show you."

Wilbur drew into himself a little at the prospect of being singled out so, and he detested the pet-man intensely as he led Wilbur through the damp and noisome quarters of protesting animals to – *what* – Wilbur didn't know.

They entered a dark and awesomely quiet room. Wilbur, though he could see nothing clearly, could feel, all around him, a multitude of presences and could hear a low undercurrent of sound, of vague rustlings and breathing. Their entrance had occasioned a slight stirring all about, like the momentary throbbing of a heartbeat. In the farthest corner there was a cage, dimly lit and apparently empty except for the outline of a circle within.

"*Voila*, here it is," said the pet-man.

"Here is what?" asked Wilbur, bewildered, for he could see nothing but the emptiness of space in the void of the cage.

"Why, here is the marvelous thing of which I spoke, *Monsieur*," said the pet-man, pointing toward the circle in the cage.

Wilbur approached the cage stealthily, frightened of the nothingness before him.

"But there is nothing here," he said, turning on his heels to the pet-man in exasperation.

"*Exactly*, *Monsieur*, the very latest thing in pets, for the man of fashion, such as yourself. A hole."

"A *hole*?" cried Wilbur, drawing the printed handkerchief once more from his pocket.

"But of course, *Monsieur*," said the pet-man, excited. "Just imagine, a pet that requires nothing, because it *is* nothing. The perfect pet for a busy man like yourself."

Wilbur drew back a step or two and looked at the cage. All he could see was a dimly glowing circle, like a shimmering halo of light, slightly pulsating, at the center of which was the darkened outline of the hole.

Yes, he mused in his distractedly thoughtful way, it was a good-looking hole, perfectly circular, without a flaw.

"Well, *Monsieur*?" said the pet-man in a peculiarly soft voice.

"Oh, give me a minute, will you?" snapped Wilbur, waving him away. "It isn't every day one makes a decision like this. The least you could do is step back a little and let me think."

"Of course, *Monsieur*, we understand." Though he couldn't really see him, he could feel the pet-man smiling at him, could see in his mind's eye how he must be smiling his little wormy smile right now. And then he heard once more the vague stirrings of the unseen beasts around him, moving heavily about in their prisons; and suddenly he could smell them also, not really a noxious smell, but a thick and rather moist and heavy odor which seemed to hang in the air like smoke or fog, just unpleasant enough so that he guessed he wasn't trapped somewhere in a dream or nightmare, after all, as he had begun to wonder.

As he stood contemplating this, a soft, whirring sound began emanating from the cage, undulating toward him, wrapping itself around him like a snake. And there was something very warm and engulfing about it, this sound, like the siren moan of a lonely, begging, beckoning woman.

"Why, *Monsieur*, the thing is quite *attracted* to you," said the pet-man fervidly. "No doubt it senses your *simpatico* disposition toward it."

Wilbur looked at it again, intently, straining his eyes to see in the dimness. Why a hole? he asked himself again. Why? Something which requires nothing and, in return, gives nothing to which one need respond.

He took one more look at the hole, its siren whistle ringing in his ears, and fell hopelessly in love with it.

"Ah, *Monsieur*, you have not disappointed me," said the pet-man, gingerly ringing up the sale on the cash register. "You are, as I thought, a man of exquisite judgment."

Wilbur looked uneasily about him. The glare of light in the front room was almost intolerable after the darkness.

"I hope," he said, "that you will see fit to be discreet about this. I mean, getting a *hole* for a pet is, after all, a rather personal matter."

"Oh, indeed," said the pet-man, smiling his lubricious smile at Wilbur one last time. "We quite understand such things. It is our business, fitting the right person with just the right pet."

Wilbur carried his hole home in an apparently empty cage, becoming more and more elated with each step, his heart pounding, his blood throbbing and singing in his veins, his entire body quivering in a state of ecstasy much like that of the great, warm rush of orgasm.

He strolled jauntily down the street, prancing almost, gently swinging the cage, to and fro, by his side and looking eagerly into the faces of those who passed him for some hint of reaction, some tell-tale sign of jealousy or admiration or astonishment. But the captivated throngs brushed past him unconcernedly, as though he were nothing

66

more than a natty little man whisking an empty cage down the street.

The hole adjusted remarkably well to life in Wilbur's apartment. He quartered it in the spare bedroom, setting the cage on the blue and purple Persian rug in front of the dresser, thinking, rather imaginatively, that the thing might enjoy gazing at its reflection in the mirror during the long hours of his absence each day.

It was, after all, a very young hole and, therefore, playful.

And it was also a very hungry hole.

"But what on earth does a hole eat?" Wilbur had asked.

"Oh, just anything and everything," replied the pet-man, a statement which proved to be factual in the extreme.

Each morning before he left for work, Wilbur would place in the cage remnants of the breakfast he had been in too great a hurry to eat himself, returning in the evening to find nothing left of the food other than a few crusty crumbs and a smear of jelly, perhaps. And in the long hours of the evening, he would sit curled up before the cage, gleefully thrusting through the bars tiny tidbits of food which were quickly sucked up into some unseen gullet, accompanied by a gurgling sound of contentment.

Even after this pleasure had run its course and the hole was apparently satisfied, Wilbur would remain seated on the purple fringe of the rug, watching the hole in its subsiding movements until his eyes

67

became blinded and dizzy with the striving to see it.

Wilbur quickly learned to read its moods, which were frequent and intense, surprisingly enough for a hole. He knew when it was agitated or upset, for it became the merest whirling outline in the cage, a condition which drove Wilbur to a frenzy of solicitude. At such times he would pace nervously up and down before the cage, wringing his hands and sighing.

"Oh, my dear, dear hole," he would moan. "What have I done to offend you? Are you ill? Are you feverish? Oh, my dear, dear hole."

It didn't take long to discover, however, that on these occasions all that would soothe the hole was food, and Wilbur gave it all he had, sometimes himself going without, to pacify the nothing in the cage. The hole consumed and consumed, the food disappearing into some invisible mouth in the center, only to reappear a moment later in the bloated bulges of the outline. It had a particular penchant for little morsels of rumaki, which it slurped up greedily, toothpicks and all, not to mention countless pounds of kielbasa and bratwurst and innumerable loaves of Black Forest bread from the delicatessen around the corner.

Its tastes were quite international.

Of course, all this headlong incontinence had its consequences, for the hole grew greater and greater, until it had outgrown its original cage. Wilbur was forced to remove the bed from the spare room, to make space for the new and larger cage, which had had to be custom-built, there being none of that size to be found in any of the local pet shops.

"Now you must really begin cutting down," Wilbur would say in a mock-stern voice, while delicately offering a crisp, golden butterfly shrimp. "We don't want to be getting too round around the middle, do we?" and he'd roll on the floor with laughter, delighted with his own good humor.

All through the day, thoughts of the hole jabbed at his consciousness like a prickling needle. "I must stop on the way home and pick up some marinated eggs," he mused, while listening with one disinterested ear to his secretary's frantic pleadings about missed appointments and supervisory memos. Important letters malingered in the wire basket on his desk as he sat fretting over the setting of the thermostat in the apartment, for the hole was acutely sensitive to warmth, thriving in a temperature which made Wilbur's teeth chatter.

No one among his acquaintances knew of the hole's existence, though they had suspected for many months – even before his acquiring the hole – that there was something going on in Wilbur's life which they were not privy to. He behaved like a man dying of a disease which he doesn't wish to speak of. For a while, friends and cohorts had rallied to his aid, urging him out into society again, trying to cure his strange malaise with noise and drink and mindless hilarity.

But he had resisted, and they soon fell away.

Except for one friend, Vera Smalltap, an elegant and sophisticated lady of thirty-five, with whom he had been close for a number of years. "Wilbur, what in the world is this thing which you have contrived for me to see?" she asked.

"Hush, Vera, you'll see soon enough," said Wilbur, tingling at the prospect of revealing the hole to anyone, even Vera.

They were climbing the stairs to his apartment, having lately consumed so many martinis in a downtown bar that Wilbur had embarked irreversibly on a course he never would have considered in more sober moments. He would introduce Vera to the hole. She was his closest friend, perhaps his only friend – not counting the hole, of course.

And now, when she was numb with joy, she took his arm and pressed it to her bosom. She had not seen him for many weeks, during which time his absence had been an unfathomable anguish to her. She had wanted to call out to him, to reach out, but instead she had waited, graciously and patiently, for some sign or signal, which now, apparently, he was offering.

"Oh, Wilbur," she crooned, giggling for the first time in twenty years, "you're so utterly unpredictable. What have you done all this time I haven't seen you, written a novel or painted a great masterpiece? How like you to come up with something unexpected."

He stopped on the topmost stair and grasped her by both arms. She thought she noticed a peculiar gleam in his eyes, a reflection of the hallway light perhaps.

"Oh, Vera, it's so much better than that," he whispered hoarsely. "So much better than a painting or a book or anything you can imagine. And I wouldn't show it to anyone but you, Vera, darling."

He squeezed her arms until they hurt, and when she looked at him, it seemed for a chilling instant that he was wearing a hideous mask.

Then he laughed and brought her back to life.

"Just prepare to be astonished," he said lightly.

When they entered the apartment, it was dark, and dense with silence. The curtains were drawn shut so that not even the light from the street shone through.

Vera stood just inside the door, sniffing peevishly at the air, which was redolent of stale food and pipe tobacco and some other, queerer smell which she was unable to recognize. "Wilbur, for God's sake, turn on the light," she pleaded, and suddenly she realized how damp and chill the air lay on her skin.

"Close your eyes," he said softly, gently pulling her along by the fingertips, leading her, stumbling, into the bedroom.

"*Voila*, here it is," he said, switching on the overhead light.

Vera opened her eyes and stared into the cage, just as the hole began to whir and hum.

"Ummmm," went the hole, like a meditating monk, the sound becoming louder and more intense as the hole whirled about in the cage in a sudden frenzy.

Vera fell back against the wall, her face a perfect picture of horrified surprise. Her eyes bulged, and her lips moved, but whatever sound she was struggling to make, died in her throat.

Wilbur took one look at her, glimpsed her pantomime of horror, and abruptly pulled her from the room and shut the door.

She stumbled about the living room in a drunken panic, clicking on the lights, then threw herself onto the sofa and buried her face in her hands.

Her shoulders rose and fell, heaving as though she were sobbing, but still there was no sound.

"What is it?" she asked in a croaking whisper, suddenly looking up at him.

Wilbur stood paralyzed, staring at her mutely; then he glanced at the door behind which his pet was softly humming now.

"What *is* that thing?" she screamed, and when he turned to her once more he saw that her face was pale and bloodless.

"Vera, Vera, Vera, there's nothing to be frightened of," he said, plunging to his knees before her. "Oh, it's the loveliest thing, Vera, when you get to know it."

He took both her hands in his and held them tightly.

"What is it?" she repeated in a low voice.

"Why, it's my pet, Vera. My hole."

She gazed into his face a moment, as though trying to recognize him; then, closing her eyes, she slowly shook her head from side to side, like someone flinging off a painful memory.

"Oh, Vera, I've been so lonely," he said, almost whining. "I've felt such a terrible, aching gap in my soul. And the hole has cured that, you know."

"But what about your job, Wilbur, and your friends?" She wheeled around to face him. "What about *me*?" She drew herself up into a rigid stance, breathing slowly in and out in a visible effort to regain her composure. But when she spoke again, her voice was quiet and uncertain.

"Oh, Wilbur, don't you realize how much you have? Success in your profession..."

"Hah."

"...and financial security..."

"Hah."

He rose from the floor, where he had been kneeling like a pathetic penitent, and drew a sweeping landscape in the air with his hand.

"I'll tell you what I have," he said his mouth twisted in a knot of bitterness. "I have printed sheets on my bed and martinis for lunch and a private secretary who nags me from morning till night in her awful, wheedling voice. And I have credit cards and bosses and friends who only love me when I'm feeling on top of the world.

"And now I also have my beloved hole."

He extended his arms to her in a gesture which begged for understanding. "Oh, the hole is marvelous, Vera. You'll see."

She closed her eyes and sighed.

"Wilbur, I think you're insane."

But she could not stay away. After overcoming her initial dismay about the hole, she settled into an attitude of quiet, almost martyred understanding, which was her nature. And it was a great relief to Wilbur, to have just *one* other person know of the hole's existence.

For the first time in months, he began making tentative little forays into the social world once more, like a man cautiously dipping one toe into an icy stream. He was even daring enough to try entertaining again in the grand old manner, with cocktails and caviar and, of course, Vera always conspicuously by his side, tenaciously clinging, as though she somehow sensed this were all like the last party aboard a sinking ship.

But it was no good having guests at the apartment, for Wilbur of necessity spent most of the evening stealthily retreating to the spare room armed with fresh supplies of the expensive, catered *hors d'oeuvres* and making comforting speeches to the hole, which loudly voiced its resentment of the guests' intrusion into its sacred domain with a long, low whistling sound clearly communicated to the living room.

"Wilbur, what in heaven's name is that ungodly noise?" asked Toby Simpkins one evening after dinner, when twelve or so guests were lounging about in a gin-induced stupor.

Wilbur choked on his vermouth.

"Oh, didn't you know, Toby?" said Vera, slightly hysterically. "Wilbur's taken up a fascinating new hobby."

"And what would *that* be?" asked the skeptical Toby.

"It *just* so happens," she said, with all the dignity she could muster, "that Wilbur has acquired a very rare tape of the mating call of the African gazelle, which he has been running from the bedroom for your entertainment and enlightenment."

The guests, strange to tell, accepted this story wholly and unquestioningly – perhaps because of the amount of gin they had ingested – but still it grated on Wilbur's nerves, and he soon gave up the at-home parties.

But it was no good trying to go out for entertainment either. Standing before the bedroom mirror, humming as he struggled with his tie and feeling a little bubble of excitement working somewhere deep within his chest, he would begin to hear the whining emanating from the other room, gradually increasing in intensity. His spirits would drop with a sudden, heavy thud and he would know he was undone again.

"Damn you!" he shouted one night. "Can't you give me any peace?"

The whining abruptly ceased, which set a siren of alarm ringing in Wilbur's head. He rushed into the other room to find that the hole had dissolved into a tiny ball and was rocking, like a frightened child, back and forth, back and forth.

"Oh, my God," cried Wilbur, and he threw himself onto the floor before the cage and grasped the bars with both hands. "Please forgive me. Of course, I won't leave you. Of course, I won't."

And he didn't.

Perhaps understandably, Vera came to the apartment less and less often, though she compensated for her physical absence with an endless stream of phone calls.

"You really shouldn't confine yourself too much, Willy dear. Everyone is wondering why you come out so seldom. And, of course, I need you to bolster me, Willy, dearest," she purred with moist and poignant tenderness.

But it was too late now, for Wilbur had become the doting parent of the hole.

He found himself trapped between his love for Vera, prodded into full bloom by her recent, frantic efforts to reach him on a purely sensual level, and his attachment to the hole, which was apparently all-consuming. And he was faced anew with the problem of providing more space for it, as it had outgrown even the new cage, thanks, in part, to its latest taste, for scampi and

76

stuffed cabbage, which Wilbur lovingly had imported from a Spanish restaurant. Finally, he faced the problem in the only way he could, by tearing out the wall between the spare room and the kitchen, and turning over all the space to the hole, without a cage. (It would have been a difficult and embarrassing matter to have a cage of sufficient size built.)

The apartment was a mess now, a chaotic congestion from end to end, and he dared not have anyone enter it, except Vera, who would no longer come. He began to lie awake at night, shivering in a cold sweat and imagining countless lurid scenes in which the landlord stormed red-faced through the door to find his swell apartment ripped apart and practically disemboweled by the hole. What would he say? What *could* he say?

He could only picture himself standing, amidst all the chaos, repeating, "Well, you see I seem to have this hole... well, you see I seem to have this... well, you seem I seem to have..."

And what would happen to him upon this discovery? Worse yet, what would happen to the hole? Would they cart it away in a gigantic van to some special impounding area for overgrown pets, where it would be gassed after a few days grace, or starved and beaten? Or would they imprison it in a zoo, for people to see or not see?

He had grown very pale and thin now and was, of course, nervous almost to the point of exhaustion. Vera, also, had undergone a change for the worse. Her naturally gay demeanor had changed to one of desperate pleading, of deep, silent pain which showed through in the leaden cast of her eyes, which had once been so brilliant.

"Willy, you must come to grips with the situation," she would say, almost crying. "You must simply get rid of that thing, before it devours you, as it devours everything else which gets in its way."

"Nonsense, Vera. The hole loves me. It would never harm me."

Still, he could not deny that he had begun to feel a little shudder of apprehension each time he opened the door to enter his own apartment. For it was always a new surprise to see to what incredible degree the hole had grown and what artifacts of his life it had gobbled up during the day. It was no longer a hole in the strictest sense of the word; its girth was wound around the corners and shoved through the doorways until the apartment was almost completely a mass (or lack of mass) of it.

It was on the last day before the first anniversary of his acquiring the hole that Vera issued her ultimatum. "But, darling, you can't *mean* that," he moaned in a voice dredged up from some bottomless pit of despair. "How will I go on without you?"

"I don't know how you will go on, Wilbur," she said without emotion, "except that you *will* go on without *me* unless you get rid of that... that *thing*."

She tried to light a cigarette with trembling hands, the flame from the match illuminating the sudden crumbling of her face. "Oh, Wilbur, do you know what it's like to compete with a hole? If it were only another woman, I'd know what to do. But a *hole*, Wilbur, a *hole*."

"Please, Vera," he whined, "just give me one more chance. I'll do something about the hole. I promise. I'll... I'll board it in a kennel, I'll send it to obedience school, I'll..."

"Oh, Wilbur," she screamed, jumping up from her chair and nearly overturning the table. "You poor, pathetic fool, you idiot!"

"Vera, please don't leave me. I love you, I need you," he whimpered as he watched her scurrying between the tables to the door.

He answered Vera's ultimatum, not directly, but through his silence, and never heard from her again.

He saw her once or twice, in the restaurant they had frequented together, and he felt a little stab of yearning for her, but it was fleeting, for all his concentration was on the hole now and how to cope with it. He was living in a kind of delirium. Soon he never left the apartment anymore but merely sat in the little corner left to him and fed the hole – indeed, he continued to feed it with a fresh zeal, as though he had just grasped something, had found the spot where he was itching and, realizing he could not reach it, enjoyed the itch. With what meager funds were left to him (his once illustrious career having been terminated) he indulged the hole in its latest fancy, for raw oysters, Wilbur enjoying them along with the hole, slurping them up out of a tall glass, cold and oily.

The hole gurgled softly, as in in reply.

One evening, about three months after their last meeting, in a fit of remorse and longing, Vera tiptoed her way up the stairs, to Wilbur's apartment and began knocking. When she received no answer, she merely knocked again. She stood at the door a long time, hardly daring to breathe and listening intently for some sound or sign of life on the other side.

But there was none, only a desperate, palpable silence.

At last she placed a shaking hand on the knob and began to slowly turn it. When she did so, it made a grinding squeal, like a rusty screw being unthreaded, as though the door had not been opened in a very long time.

She stepped across the threshold and was confronted by a thick and musty odor, an all-pervasive scent of decay. The curtains were gone from the windows so that the late afternoon sun shone through in a harsh and unrelenting glare, blinding her for a moment.

"Wilbur, are you here?" called Vera from the doorway, blinking away the tiny black spots before her eyes. "Wilbur?"

There was no reply, only the deafening silence hanging like a corpse in the cold and otherworldly air.

80

"Wilbur, *please*," she called again, feeling her heart throbbing in her throat.

Suddenly she heard a small, tinny laugh which seemed to come from very far away, as though filtered through a tunnel or from the depths of a cavern. She could see clearly now, her eyes taking in the torment of confusion in the room, and all at once she caught sight of a huge object, obese and powerful, rumbling toward her like a juggernaut out of the darkened recesses of the hallway. It came nearer and nearer, a bulbous, waddling thing, like an overblown balloon, with a face painted on, just below its small, wrinkled topknot. A tiny, grinning face it was, atop a great, swollen mountain of flesh.

"Vera, how nice to see you again," said a tiny, mouse's voice from a thin slit of mouth cut into the bulbous flesh.

"*Wilbur*, she gasped, barely able to breathe, much less to speak, "is that *you*?"

"But of course, my darling," said the grotesque giant before her in its squeaking, baby voice, "and how lovely of you to come by. Could I offer you something to eat? I'm fresh out of oysters, I regret to say, but there are still several tins of sardines and some Ritz crackers left, I believe. Oh, I heartily recommend the sardines – why, they're so good I can hardly wait to get them out of their little tin boats to eat them.

"Remember the days of Camembert and caviar," he went on excitedly, a little

81

trail of saliva running down his chin, which was like a fat, pink glob of clay stuck on the bottom of his face, "and those magnificent escargots at Antoine's which seemed to simply slide down your throat like they were running down a river? And the frog's legs at Pierre's and Luigi's cannelloni and..."

"Wilbur, *Wilbur*," she said in a harsh, low whisper, "where is the hole?"

"Well, I have come on hard times lately, you know," said the globular protuberance before her in a whining, petulant voice.

"Wilbur, what has happened to the *hole*?" she cried, her eyes bulging in disbelief at all she saw. "What have you done with the *hole*?"

"Why, Vera, darling," he squealed, "I *ate* it, of course."

*Originally published In the May 1977 issue of *Gallery Magazine*.

5 <u>LILLIAN'S VOICE</u>

Mr. Kroger didn't so much *move* to Sylvan Court as simply wake up there one day, a bit of logistical magic accomplished by Ernest The Plumber, who was Mr. Kroger's son.

"Just think," said Ernest, waving a sheaf of colored brochures before the old man's face, "no more putting up with the kids or the dog or Sylvia's cooking. Just good old peace and quiet for yourself."

Mr. Kroger sensed that he was about to be swooped up by Fate and so leaned forward in his rocking chair, pushing Tennyson aside in his mind to formulate a vague protest. But then he noticed the fire in his son's eyes and the way the sun glistened along his stout, hairy arms, and he sank back. He wondered briefly, looking into Ernest's dark, flushed face, how his son had managed to steal all his white-hot energy to keep for himself. Not that he begrudged him. No, indeed.

"And you don't ever have to leave your room, if you don't want to," Ernest continued in a warm gush of words, "because everything you need is right there, color TV, massage shower, a panel of buttons on the wall to control the temperature and even — get this - a bed that jiggles you to sleep each night."

It seemed to Mr. Kroger that he was just

about to make the point that he did not *want* to be jiggled to sleep when he suddenly found himself in a pale green cubicle of a room, alone with all that remained to him of worldly gain, a ragged suitcase stuffed with clothing and a dusty carton of books. Gone, suddenly, was the musty, creaking mattress in the corner room of Ernest's house; gone the sagging bookshelves and the row of faded pictures on the wall; gone the fragrant, summer yard alive with insects and the sound of children.

Looking all around him, he could not find a single thing he knew, no well-aged artifacts or chipped reminders of the past or even any friendly dust. Just sterile newness everywhere.

"*Kids*," he muttered with unmistakable indictment, referring, of course to Ernest, who was forty-two years old and as childlike as a battle cruiser. Then he lit a cigarette with shaking hands and dropped the first ash to the floor.

He was sitting on the porch of Sylvan Court, one glazed afternoon, still trying to gulp down his dismay, when he felt a feather touch upon his knee.

"Do pardon me. You're turning a little pink, you know, and my sister and I wondered if you wouldn't be more comfortable here in the shade?"

Mr. Kroger looked up to find two silvery ladies sitting just across from him in a kind of shaded nook on the edge of the tiled porch.

The one who had spoken was still leaning toward him with her butterfly fingers giving one last, convulsive flutter for his attention. Even sitting in the chair, slumped forward like a piece of fallen baggage, she looked tall and angular and brittle — one could almost see the rusty wires, bending inside her bones, as she moved - and her craggy face was swallowed in a smile.

The other woman was small and round and delicate, a little plump, perhaps, still melting down from youthfulness. A trace of teasing girlhood twinkled in the corners of her bow mouth. She extended a crepe paper hand in silent greeting, two blue pools of eyes blinking mischievously.

"'Afternoon, ladies," said Mr. Kroger in his best gentleman's manner. "I'm Walter Kroger, at your service." He dragged his metal chair along the tiles and settled snugly next to the blue eyes, enchanted.

"*We* are Lillian Crenshaw," said the lady with the craggy face, nodding toward her sister, "and I am Myrtle. We are very pleased to meet you, I'm sure."

Lillian gave a queer little nod of her head then, a quite emphatic motion in the direction of the lounge.

"My sister wonders if you wouldn't like to have something cool to drink," said Myrtle, "while we pass the time of day?"

Lillian pursed her lips and blew out a long breath, waving the crepe paper hand in front of her face like a fan.

"...especially as it seems so fiercely warm this afternoon," added Myrtle, taking up the point as if on cue.

Mr. Kroger experienced a fleeting sensation of being at the United Nations, listening to the translation of a speech. "Might as well," he said. "Can't say as I've any pressing business to attend to."

He flagged down a blue-coated waiter, a young man he had seen snickering, at the passing white heads of Sylvan Court, and ordered lemonades all around.

"And how do you like it here?" he asked Lillian's blue eyes, allowing his long hand to linger dangerously near her own.

She gave her head a quick shake of affirmation and looked at him with a smile which drifted down to sadness.

"Oh, we like it just fine," intruded Myrtle once more. "It's very comfortable and clean. Of course, it can be lonely," she said, gazing at Lillian and squinting, like someone reading fine print, "to feel so cut off, you know, so isolated, as though we have to be kept out of sight and not remind the younger generation what's in store for them."

This was the first hint Mr. Kroger had that others shared his sense of exile in this place. In his room and in the pastel corridors and even here, on the sun-speckled porch, he felt as far away from Ernest and Sylvia and the children as time and miles could make him. And Emily not here to ease the pain, he thought, scolding her in his mind for having died before him.

He leaned forward in his chair, bowed by the weight of memory until his shoulder grazed the filmy fabric of Lillian's dress. She smelled exactly as the lace in his mother's drawer had smelled in that gentle, ancient time when he was a boy.

He looked up with new eyes, unburdened suddenly. "But surely there's no need to feel lonely when we have each other," he blurted. "I mean, it isn't all that bad to be among one's peers at our age, is it?"

Lillian frowned, the merest shadow of petulant regret clouding her face. She turned to her sister with a dark nod and Myrtle took up the challenge.

"Still, it isn't easy to grow old," she sighed, "especially if one has lived a very full and vibrant life, as Lillian has. She had the whole world at her feet, you know, when she was young."

"Why, yes, I can imagine," said Mr. Kroger, somewhat startled. "Beautiful women usually do." Unwittingly, he winked, to no one, and nothing in particular - but still, he felt foolish.

Lillian touched a finger lightly to her cheek, as if to brush his wink away, and then, in a graceful, girlish gesture, she pushed the pale hair from her forehead and let her hand drift down along her chin. "Of course, *true* beauty resides in the soul," Myrtle was saying, quite inconsequentially. "It shines through at any age and under any circumstance. Don't you think?"

"But what does Lillian think?" asked Mr. Kroger. "*That* is the question." He stared into the blue eyes, defiantly, and thought he saw them do a quick little dance of amusement.

"She cannot answer you, Mr. Kroger," said Myrtle in a brown paper tone. "She lost her speech a year ago, with her stroke, you know."

Mr. Kroger felt he had been slapped. He looked, into that bright, presumptuous face, and wondered that no answering voice could come from it. "Oh, my," he said, "how terrible. How tragic."

Lillian made a darting gesture with her hands, flinging her fingers at her throat.

"Tragic, indeed," said Myrtle. "If only you had heard her sing as a young girl, you would *know* how tragic. Why, when she sang the *Ave Maria* at Christmastime, it was the high point..."

Mr. Kroger sat back, mulling how he would adjust to having no voice, now that there was no one to talk to, except himself and whatever spirits listened to the drab and repetitious musings of an old man.

"And there is nothing left?" he asked, interrupting the flow of reminiscence. "No voice at all? And yet it seems that I just talked to her."

"*I* am Lillian's voice now," said Myrtle with swelling pride. When Lillian looked up at this, vastly pleased and flickering all over like a diamond in the light, Myrtle reached out to pat her knee with bony fingers and added, "Which is not to say that Lillian is a 'dummy'."

Mr. Kroger was halfway through a hoarse chuckle when he noticed Lillian pouting and he hushed himself. There was here, as in Ernest's yard, a fervid hum of insects and a sense of summer haze covering everything, muting color, drowning Time. One could almost reach out and hold sound and light and movement in his hand, as though the world had paused to sigh.

Though it was only Myrtle and Mr. Kroger who conversed, of course, he felt that it was Lillian he listened to. For Myrtle translated her every nod, and gesture, the slightest tremor of lip or tilt of jaw, into a waterfall of revelation.

Once, when Lillian did a giddy pantomime in her chair, batting her eyes at heaven and tapping her patent-leather toes upon the tiles, Myrtle dutifully recited the story of Lillian's leaving home at seventeen, with a rabbit's foot and a dollar, to dance in a vaudeville revue in New York City. And she would have been a great star, too, if only she hadn't twisted an ankle chasing a Pekingese down Fifth Avenue.

Mr. Kroger listened with the brave attention of a lover. Lillian, he thought, was very special, had tasted wines he'd never dreamed of in his dreary corner of the world. She had not, for one thing, wasted half a lifetime trying to make an Ernest love a single line of poetry.

"It's, 'I must go down to the *sea* again,' you… dumb ox," he heard himself shouting.

"Of course, *I* stayed home to tend to

89

Mama and the house," Myrtle was saying. "I was never the adventuress that Lillian was."

"Quite right, quite right," said Mr. Kroger ungallantly, pressing two fingers to his temple, where the hair was scarce and yellow-white.

"And have you ever been much interested in poetry?" he dared. For surely a soul as true and timorous as Lillian's knew what it was to be in love with words, as he was, drunk and stumbling from too much lovely language.

"Why, yes, of course," said Myrtle quickly, "Keats and Coleridge especially." And she and Lillian thought it was certainly true, as Emily Dickinson had averred for all time, that there was no frigate like a book.

"Ah, yes," sighed Mr. Kroger, savoring.

Then Myrtle, released from her mission a moment while Lillian sipped her drink, murmured in a voice of different texture, "Of course, there is always your 'Ship of Fools'."

Mr. Kroger, hearing, laughed in some vacant room in his mind, not wanting to unsettle Lillian's repose. The sun was a pale and ineffectual glimmer through the trees, shining in patchwork squares of frosty light upon the lawn.

"Oh, dear," said Myrtle with the startled awareness of someone waking late. "I don't know where the time has gone. We'll be late for dinner, surely."

"No, no," said Mr. Kroger. "Oh, no, no, no. There's plenty of time yet," he lied.

90

For he didn't want them to leave, he didn't want Lillian *ever* to leave.

"Well, I don't know how you can know that, Mr. Kroger, inasmuch as you're not wearing a watch." Myrtle was already gathering up a soft and woolly armful of her and Lillian's things, with brisk, intemperate authority.

"My dear lady, I don't tell time by reading clocks or watching stars," he said, looking out to the half-shell of sun on the horizon. "Each morning I stick a finger in the air and wind up the timepiece in my mind. And then I'm set for the whole day."

"Well, that is all very fine, I'm sure," laughed Myrtle, pushing herself up strenuously from her chair, "though I don't know how you stand the ticking."

Lillian, adrift for the moment, began to wave a pale, pink handkerchief before her face, which was like a shout.

Ernest came to visit on Sunday, torn like a child from its mother's bosom away from the crankshaft of his creaking truck. He brought a box of Sylvia's cookies, which Mr. Kroger shuddered to accept, and some colored drawings from the children. "Found yourself a sweetie-pie, huh, Pop?" he said, sweeping through the vapid atmosphere of Sylvan Court.

"Now, Ernest, you must mind your manners," said his father, struggling to keep in stride. "None of those jokes you hear at the plumber's union. That wouldn't do. Lillian Crenshaw is a lady of great refinement.

"...and so is her sister," he added, having forgotten Myrtle briefly, as he usually did.

They sat on the porch, the four of them, sipping drinks together while the sun played checkers on the grass. Mr. Kroger felt that there had never been another time before these afternoons he spent with Lillian, listening to the soft unraveling of her life and thoughts.

"And, of course, Lillian was intimately acquainted with the Duke of Windsor," Myrtle was saying, with a brave heave of her bony chest. "She was just going to meet him, in fact, upon an ocean liner leaving for the continent, when she bumped her head on a Dutch door at the Ritz Hotel."

Lillian sat in the shadows, subtly conducting with her hands and eyes the stream of Myrtle's narrative. A symphony, thought Mr. Kroger, and he scooted his chair a little closer and leaned forward, as though to hear her better.

"Well, I guess you two gals have been around quite a bit by now," Ernest barged in then, to Mr. Kroger's dismay.

"Oh, yes," replied Myrtle, with her head thrown back and her rocky cliff of chin raised to the dying sun, "around and around and around.

"And into corners, crevices and cracks you never dreamed of, young man. Isn't that right, Lillian?"

Lillian withheld her customary nod here, only a slight twitch of brow betraying that she'd heard.

"We have been diamonds and rubies," continued Myrtle, "and also dull stones. You cannot always shine, you know? Sometimes, indeed," she said, with a brief, sideward glance, "the best thing you can give is, not light, but a cool and merciful shade."

She seemed on the verge of saying something else, her eyes seeking in some distant hemisphere for a point of landing or a harbor in memory, when Lillian began to wave her frail wisp of handkerchief frantically.

"Of course, *Lillian* has seen and known so much more than I," she said quickly. "Why, she has lived the gay life in Paris and Rome and London, and all of the capitals of the world. And, in some lesser-known spots, as well."

"Well, it's like I always tell Pop, here," said Ernest, plunging backward in his thin, metal chair, "a town is a town, and you can be as big a numb-skull in one place as another. Isn't that right, Pop?"

Mr. Kroger felt the full force of suffocating circumstance upon him. He braved a glance at Lillian, looked up from under his frosty lashes to find her lips unfolding in a wry, discordant smile in his direction.

And there was something urgent and commanding in her face which spoke louder than any words.

"But Lillian is very special, Ernest, *very* gifted and special," he said, hearing his words like the chanting of a pre-recorded message on the telephone. She was,

93

he noticed, melting into her chair once more with a long sigh of approval.

"Hell, everybody is special," thundered Ernest, "in some way or other. Why, you take old Myrtle here..." he added, "why, I know an old soldier when I see one, someone who has been knocked down a fair number of times and got up to fight again. Ain't that right, Myrtle, honey?"

Myrtle's face took on the luminescent quality of a falling star, and just as transiently. "Well, yes, I have fought," she said, looking into her lap, "but that is not to say that I have won."

"Win, win, win," said Ernest disparagingly. "Hell, it's the *fight* that counts."

Mr. Kroger looked at Lillian and felt his heart sinking like the light in the West. She seemed very much quiet today, he thought, perhaps because her pale, blue handkerchief blended with the sky and didn't make much noise.

"That is some fine lady you got yourself there, Pop," said Ernest.

They were standing together in the lobby in the bare-bulb light of wasted evening. Ernest had thrown his denim arm around his father, taking his leave, perhaps for a while or perhaps forever, according to his whim and Sylvia's pleading.

"Yessir, they don't make 'em much better than that."

Mr. Kroger sensed that this was in the manner of a farewell or parting gesture, and so he tried to *feel* Ernest's arm across his

94

shoulder, the weight and roughness of it; he tried to cast it in the strange metal of memory as he had once cast Ernest's shoes in bronze.

He realized, suddenly and astoundingly, that all that was left of him and Emily and Ernest, was this once embrace.

"Why, yes, I'm glad you noticed that," he said, stepping away from all he had in life. He had learned as a boy, and always remembered, that it was best to be the first one to go; never linger, was the dictum, never to be the straggler calling, "Wait for me."

"She is a very special lady," he murmured, conscious only of this moment in which his son was caught in a brown and curling still-life frame, unalterable and slowly fading.

"You bet your life she is," said Ernest, taking in an irrevocable step backward. "You better latch onto her for sure. That Myrtle is really something."

"*Who?*" said Mr. Kroger, startled. "Who?" But it was too late. Ernest was gone, through the double doors, leaving only his pulsing aura in the empty rooms. "But it was *Lillian* I meant."

Mr. Kroger called upon a host of memories that night, in order not to think about what was. Emily and Ernest were gone for sure, as if they had never existed except in his mind and memory, like cold, rough-textured portraits. Life was nothing so much, he thought, as an endless and cruel

95

series of beginnings, and where did one find the strength at his age?

"You dare not blink your eyes or cross your arms," Myrtle had said only the other day, on the porch, "for fear it will all pass away before you've had a chance to touch it."

In his despair, he lay back on the too-cool, printed sheets, and tried to draw a picture of Lillian in the evanescent darkness. He got her lips, which curled and sinuated, and her plastic, darling fingers and...

"There is always something to be grateful for, at least," he remembered Myrtle saying once, as she fondled a stray cat in her lap, shivering with pleasure.

...and the shimmering blue eyes...

"What was it Tennyson said about an idle king with no more worlds to conquer?"

...and the rich, encompassing voice, which spoke as though the very key to life were in a word, and not just a word but one well-spoken, at that.

"Being Lillian's voice, this past year, has been an awesome job, you know?" he heard Myrtle saying in his uninvited recollection. "How can I ever know if I'm expressing what she really thinks and feels?"

...*Lillian's voice*.

"Lillian's voice," he hissed, sitting up in bed to stare at the blind light of midnight.

Very early the next morning, when the world was still moist and quiet, Mr. Kroger went downstairs, across the porch and out into the damp and dark green garden. He felt he hadn't slept in countless years, maybe never, and his legs carried him with a great weariness, as though they might give way at any moment.

He thought he would like to lie down in the cool grass and fall asleep and never worry anymore. But just ahead he saw a solitary figure bending to some new blossoms on the fence.

"Good morning, Myrtle," he said, taking in a deep and pungent breath of morning air, which revived him.

"Why, Mr. Kroger, you're up awfully early this morning, aren't you?"

"Yes, I thought I'd find you here at this time, from what you said." He looked around, among the trees and flowering bushes, to the end of the brown lane, and spoke softly, "Where is Lillian?"

"Oh, gracious," laughed Myrtle, "Lillian is still upstairs, sleeping as soundly as a babe." She looked at the flowers she was holding and rubbed one finger lightly on its velvety smoothness. "This is the only time I have to myself, you know, *really* to myself."

Mr. Kroger took a step forward, feeling somehow very young and very old at the same time, and placed one hand gently on her shoulder.

"Then would you like to talk a walk with me?" he asked.

6 THE SALAMANDER IN THE FIRE

All morning long a stout Cossack of a woman watched me - everything I did - until I felt I would have to leap out of bed and beat her over the head with one of the squat, ugly vases which had been brought into the room, filled with half-dead flowers. I could see her lips moving as I ate my scrambled eggs and toast, as though I needed help with the chewing. Finally, a large lump welled up in my throat and I shoved back the hospital tray with a clatter of dishes.

She stared at me disapprovingly a moment, a dark cloud knitting briefly across her pale, square face, then gathered up some knitting from her lap and began a staccato rhythm of clicking needles.

For two days she had been sitting at the bedside of her ancient mother, my roommate. But the mother slept now, taking in the air in short, noisy gasps. The old woman's cheekbones rose like chalk cliffs out of the sunken valleys of her face; her hair lay spread across the pillow in thin strands, like bits of floating seaweed.

"She's not long for it, you know," said the Cossack daughter, nodding toward the gray and shrunken head on the pillow. I thought the corners of her mouth turned down in disgust when she said this.

"I'm terribly sorry to hear that," I said, startled out of a cognizance of my own pain and sickness.

"Oh, you needn't be," she said matter-of-factually. "She hadn't been much use to anybody for a long time. Just a burden. Just a burden, to herself and to all of us. Best thing can happen is for the Lord to take her and put her out of her misery."

I looked at the old woman and imagined the Lord coming down to "Take" her, as though she were a package to be delivered somewhere.

"Yessir, best thing can happen," said the daughter, clicking the needles together furiously. "When people get to be her age they don't get too much out of life anyway. Why, she's just as helpless as a newborn baby. I been havin' to wash and dress and feed her for almost a year now — just the same as if she *was* a little baby."

Suddenly she flung both hands into her lap, the knitting crumbling into a little black pile on her skirt, and she looked up at me defiantly.

"I tell you what, she may look skinny to *you*, but you try lifting ninety-some-odd pounds every day for a year and see if it don't get you down."

She took up the knitting once more, angrily drawing out a length of yarn with her forefinger.

"But I seen these old people linger on for two, three years," she said, taking up the conversation as easily as she had taken up the knitting, "just wearin' on everybody's nerves and gettin' in everybody's way."

She gave me a dark, accusing look.

"'Course, you wouldn't know how that is 'less you ever had some old person to tend to yourself. Like I told Brother, we should have Mama put in a nursing home a long time ago. She would know no difference anyway."

Her eyes closed into a half-moon slit as she looked down upon the noisy, stinting labor of her knitting.

"But won't you miss her awfully when she's gone?" I asked wonderingly, for I had come to know this old woman, even in her stillness.

Occasionally, she had spoken to me, in her infrequent waking moments, saying, "Child, don't never take nothin' for granted, don't never throw away what you can't ever get back again."

She mostly mumbled and murmured, it is true, but there did seem to be something she was trying to say.

"Oh, hon," her daughter was saying, "I don't expect I'll ever have time to be missing anybody. I got about a year's worth of work to catch up on. You know, it's like the Holy Book says, the Lord giveth and the Lord taketh away, and it ain't none of our business when He gives or takes."

For some reason her words made me feel weak and uneasy. I closed my eyes and for a frightening moment, I felt I was lying in the other bed, my hands losing their grip on the last, slippery thread of life.

"You can only live so long anyways," I heard her saying, "and then you have to give way to the younger folk. We ain't meant to live too long, you know, and she's already outlived her usefulness. Outlived two sons who died in the wars and outlived a daughter who died 'a cancer at age thirty-one, and outlived my daddy, God rest his soul."

She knitted a moment in silence, and it occurred to me that she might be thinking of all those lives, which had come and gone while hers went on. But then she dropped the knitting from one hand and pulled the perspiration from her forehead with short, blunt fingers. "*Dang* that doctor," she said fiercely, "I got cornbread to make."

I began to wonder where I had seen this woman before. I was sure I had seen her a hundred times in a hundred different bodies — in the supermarket and the Laundromat and stomping righteously down the steps of the Four-Square Church on Sunday mornings, her formidable bosom heaving with satisfaction. But there was something else she reminded me of also, from a different time and place. Though she was big-boned and heavy, her head was amazingly small, with eyes like shiny beads. Suddenly I thought of that creature which can crawl through fire and emerge unscathed, unaffected. In her face was the same remote, primeval look.

On the bed, the old woman began to moan and lifted a trembling hand to her daughter, her crepe-paper eyelids flickering open.

But the milky-white eyes that were revealed looked glazed and sightless.

"Sonny, is that you? Is that you, Sonny?" Her voice was a cracked whisper.

"Now, Mama, you know well as anything that Sonny's not here," said her daughter loudly. "He's home, where he should be."

She turned to me and hissed conspiratorially, "Sonny's her great-grandson, eleven years old. She thinks he done set the moon and stars."

"I want to see Sonny," the old woman moaned. "Where's my Sonny boy?"

Her daughter leaned forward and began to slap the foot of the bed with a broad, freckled hand.

"Now, Mama, you just go back to sleep. You know well as anything that Sonny's mother and daddy's not about to let him come up here to this hospital," she laughed. "Why, that little fella 'd be scared to death to come to this place."

She continued to look at the small, white face on the pillow, but without seeing to see it. Then she pursed her lips and frowned.

"Why on *Earth* don't that doctor never come when he's s' posed to? I got better things to do, than sit here waitin' for some fool doctor to show up."

There was a sudden movement in the bed, a rising and falling. And then, a harsh and ghastly sound, which seemed to be rising out of some deep and bottomless cavern.

When I looked at the old woman, I was astonished. She was crying: great, wrenching sobs which shook her frail body. And yet the glazed eyes were dry.

"My God," I groaned, "she's *crying.*"

"Oh, don't you pay no attention to that," said the daughter. "That's the way these old people will do. Why, they don't know *what* they're doing, half the time."

She made dizzingly little circles, with the knitting needles, and looked reprovingly at her mother out of the corners of her eyes.

But the rough, grating sound of the old woman's sobbing filled the room, until I thought my ears would burst from it. I could not bear to watch her shriveled body heaving on her deathbed, and so I turned away. Outside, the leaves were turning brown and red and blowing to the ground, were being buried in a mass graveyard of dead leaves. There were so many of them, heaping leaf after leaf on the mass funeral mound.

Just then the old woman emitted a long and desperate moan - it must have been dredged up, painfully, from the very bottom of her soul.

"*Do* something," I pleaded, plagued by my own ephemeral pain and the pervading sense of final and unremitting loss voiced in the old woman's cry.

The clicking needles stopped and the woman bent forward to her mother. "Now, Mama, you just hush that, you hear? You're scaring the life outta this poor woman over here." She darted a quick, humorous glance at me, then reared back her head and began to laugh hoarsely.

The old woman's hand shook like a butterfly in the air and fluttered to rest on the bed. Her fingers were crooked like talons, and her long granite nails dug into the white sheet at her side. But gradually the crying subsided into the short, whining sobs of a baby, and then, finally, she was quiet and still again.

"Sonny," she whispered once, and then the thin, transparent sheath of her lids drew shut, locking her into a dark unconsciousness.

"That's a good girl, that's a good girl," intoned her daughter. "You just be still there and don't give us no more trouble."

She looked at me and laughed, her thin slit of a mouth drawn downward even in laughter.

"Now, isn't she just a case?" she said, and slapped the bed once more for good measure.

I looked at her shiny, beady eyes, which were remnants of the Ice Age: cold, unknowing, dumb and pitiful. "*Salamander*," I thought, remembering suddenly, and turned to watch the dead leaves dropping on the ground.

7 THE PERFECT ROBOT BABY*

It had the rosiest cheeks. And it had the curliest dark brown hair, almost black, in fact, falling in perfectly spiraled ringlets down its forehead and over its two, little china-cup ears. The bluest of sea-blue eyes stared out of its pink, baby-fat face. When Mrs. Harding reached out a hand to it, five plump fingers entwined about her thumb, squeezing with a gentle pressure, and a soft calf-like cooing gurgled from its throat.

Mrs. Harding cooed back in response, making such a low, alien sound that her husband looked at her with astonishment.

"Oh, it's perfect," she gasped in the same strange voice. "I mean, *he* is – or *she*. Which is it?"

"Whichever you prefer," said Manager crisply. "This model comes in either sex, as they all do. The same basic design with an alteration or two to distinguish male from female. There's really not that much difference, you know."

"Oh, Walter, which shall we have?" said Mrs. Harding, turning to her husband. "A boy or a girl?"

Before he could answer, she bent her head down and softly clucked at the Botticelli face turned upside to hers. The plump fingers tightened their grip about her thumb and then, with a brilliance which lit up the room, the rosebud lips parted, opening into a wide smile.

"Oh, Walter, I say, which shall we *have*?" she asked desperately. For all that it mattered, she knew she must have one, or even *all* of them, everyone that her arms and heart could hold.

Mr. Harding leaned back, crossed his arms and blew a stray lock of graying hair from his temple. "Well, I must leave that decision entirely up to you, dear. After all, you are the one who will be caring for it." He winked at Manager, whose face remained as a passive as a hundred-year-old glacier. "But Manager says there's really not that much difference between the two."

"Oh, I *can't* decide," agonized Mrs. Harding, still staring into the pearly-pink face in the showcase cubicle. Suddenly she drew her hand away, as though it were being scorched, and turned to the others with a pleading expression.

"Perhaps I can be of some assistance in this matter of sex," said Manager, taking a step forward. "We have found through research involving countless cases that clients of your type – that is, middle-aged and upper middle-class, who have never had a child of their own, are much more adaptable to the *female* gender." Manager paused to smile, a short twitch of a smile, while the Hardings looked at each other as though they had just learned who they are. "The *female* gender," went on Manager, "poses fewer and less difficult problems than does the male.

106

Youthful energy and stamina are required to deal with the male, a constant physical vigilance which might prove altogether too strenuous for people your age."

The Hardings once again exchanged glances and sighed in unison, as if from exhaustion or despair.

"Whereas the female," continued Manager, "requires only the wisdom of maturity, a stubborn conscience on your part, and a bit of intimidation now and then, which comes naturally to parents of all ages.

"And so," said Manager in a voice which seemed to put the matter to rest, "shall we place your order for a girl?"

Mrs. Harding peered into the showcase at the tiny, bobbing head, still smiling sweetly up at her. "Oh, couldn't we just take this one," she sighed, "whichever it is?"

"This one? Why, this one is nothing, merely a model," laughed Manager and proceeded to lift the bunting and toss it back against the wall, where it landed with a clunk.

The Hardings named the baby girl Melissa, after Mr. Harding's mother, long since dead. They called her Missy, however, obeying that strange and universal inclination to call others by any but their own true names. She was a replica of the child they had seen in in the showcase except that underneath the swaddling clothes

107

she possessed the distinguishing accouterments of an infant female. None of which mattered, of course, because she was everything they had ever wanted, simply, by virtue of being a baby, their very own, as sweet and plump and dimpled, as soft and round and pink, as one could ask for. To their every gesture, word and look she responded with a gurgle of contentment, a little bubble of happiness bursting on her lips. Mrs. Harding cooed at her for hours and marveled when the tiny fingers gripped her in a kind of speechless communication then, while Mr. Harding could not pass the high chair or crib or playpen without reaching down to ruffle the soft brown hair. When he did that, he felt ten feet tall, as if he had begotten a thousand babies with his own prolific seed.

Of course, the routine of life in the Harding household altered rather drastically with the purchase of the robot baby. Mr. Harding no longer returned from work in the evenings to find his wife greeting him at the door with a comforting smile and a freshly mixed martini. Instead, she was more likely to be found in the kitchen concocting some curious mixture for the lifelike baby's dinner, or else in the nursery changing linen and picking up what seemed an inordinate amount of refuse left over from the day's activities.

Walking down the hallway in search of her, Mr. Harding would often stumble over rubber toys that squeaked indignantly when stepped on, plastic rattles, and even, occasionally, a rather frayed and disreputable-looking copy of Dr. Spock. When found at last, though, Mrs. Harding would be all aglow with maternal satisfaction, if a little unkempt for someone of her fastidiousness, and for a blessed moment Mr. Harding would lean over the frilly crib and tickle the chin of his very own baby girl before the minuscule computer in her set itself to "Sleep".

She seemed perfection in every way, "worth every cent," as Mr. Harding liked to say teasingly to his wife, who no longer expressed the same appreciation of his humor as in former days. Through some miraculous marriage of science and ingenuity, Missy's growth and development exactly paralleled those standards set down in the authoritative "child behavior" books, with no sign or sound of the delicate machinery ceaselessly at work within her. At six months the first pearl of a tooth appeared.

By the time she was eighteen months old she was toddling through the house, knocking over vases and bookends and generally leaving a trail of debris in her path. All of which the Hardings gratefully coped with, for she had by now become so much a part of their lives they quite forgot they had purchased her at a giant warehouse during an "end-of-season clearance."

Then, without warning, something went wrong. When Missy was barely two years old (that is, when she had been *operational* for two years), Mr. Harding returned one evening to find his wife in a state of near hysteria, babbling incoherently and flinging her arms about at several scenes of senseless chaos – a confusion of scattered toys and books and papers and upended tables – as though a twister had lifted the house up and let it drop to the ground again.

"She's been a *horror* today," Mrs. Harding cried, wringing her hands and panting like a sprinter. "She refused to eat her dinner, she broke my favorite Aztec ashtray, and when I put her in the tub for her bath, she splashed water all over me and ruined my hairdo.

"And now she won't go to sleep." Mrs. Harding collapsed on the couch in an attitude of hopelessness.

Mr. Harding stood back and surveyed the scene. "Hmmm," he mused, "must be a short circuit in her wiring. How long is her warranty good for?"

Mrs. Harding sighed as though she were expelling very soul and closed her eyes. "Eighteen years, I think," she mumbled and fell into a heavy slumber.

"I'm so distressed to hear that you've been having problems with Q-191," said Manager. "Ordinarily we get very few problems about that model. We're rather proud of it, in fact."

The Hardings were sitting tightly upright, side by side, on an imitation leather couch, while Missy, or Q-191-003B, as she was temporarily referred to, was being held in the Repair and Maintenance Department nearby. "Well, that may be," said Mr. Harding, "but surely you can see from what we've told you that something has gone terribly wrong *our* Missy – I mean *our* Q-191."

Manager's friendly visage went suddenly stern and a sheaf of printed paper was whisked from out of nowhere to flutter before their eyes.

"Perhaps," spoke Manager. "The behavioral patterns you have described, which may or may not be *problems*, depending upon how they are reacted to, fall into a particular category. The terms of your sales agreement," said Manager, waving the agreement before the Hardings' faces, "do not cover this category, which is technically known as 'two-year-old intransigence,' a minor deviation which might result in any highly complex machinery under certain 'atmospheric' conditions." Manager looked at them both with icy eyes that sent them shivering from the room.

And so, Missy was taken home unrepaired. They were unable, at this point, to get their money back or trade her in for a newer model, and besides, they had grown terribly fond of her, in spite of her defects. Mrs. Harding gasped less audibly and desperately when she saw her favorite mementos crashing to the floor in tiny bits and pieces. "They're only *things*," she said, "nothing lasts forever." Mr. Harding, for his part, seemed to take it all in stride until the

Saturday morning when he awoke to find that Missy had converted his prized blue angora sweater into a blanket for her Baby-Wetem doll.

On such occasions, he and Mrs. Harding would stare at each other and rush to pull the warranty from the dresser drawer, only to discover that the latest malfunction was conspicuously missing from the list of those covered by their sales agreement.

"But it can't be!" Mrs. Harding would cry out in despair. "They promised she'd be perfect."

In some ways she was. She continued to delight them with the gentle unfolding of her bud-like beauty year after year, and with the depth of her affection and attachment to them, which seemed to grow stronger with each passing day. Whenever they least expected it, when they were the most distraught over the recent machinations of her faltering machinery, she would throw two deliciously soft, plump arms about their necks and press her warm and blushing cheek against their own.

"Oh, Mama," she would whisper, "Oh, Daddy," causing any memory of the latest aberrations to float away on a hazy cloud of contentment.

But there were times, interspersed among years of fretful happiness, when her actions and attitude became so inexplicably deranged that they could only think something had gone terribly awry in her inner workings. Surely there was some nut or bolt or screw which could be tightened, some wire come loose, some simple, mechanical adjustment which would set her right again.

When she was five, for instance, she set fire to the garbage cans, sending an unholy stench floating out across the neighborhood. When she was seven, she hid in the attic for six hours with her dog, until the terror-stricken Hardings had sent for the police, the Highway Patrol, and were on the verge of calling in the FBI. And when she was nine, she dug a deep, rutty hole, amidst Mrs. Harding's backyard rose garden, uprooting the delicate plants and flinging dirt over the finely manicured lawn.

"I was going to China," Missy declared in an abrasively squeaky voice that could only have been the result of a breakdown in the voice-box chamber.

Once again, she was taken to the factory to be examined, oiled, adjusted, while the Hardings fidgeted on Manager's imitation leather couch. "This is the *second* time you have brought her here," said Manager in a solemn voice, unsmiling. "The first time, I indulged you in your inexperienced parenthood. But now, I wonder. Can you be so displeased that you would cast her away from you, into the junk pile of discarded objects?"

"But she isn't right," insisted Mr. Harding while Mrs. Harding nodded.

"Perhaps it is *you* who are not right," Manager spoke with glinting anger, and strode from the room without a backward glance.

So, they took her home once more, bemoaning the fact that she could not be fixed, nor all their efforts and expense be compensated for.

In spite of it all, she grew and thrived, dispensing pleasure and only intermittently setting the siren alarm ringing in her parents' breasts, so that all thoughts of the factory were set aside, not entirely forgotten but held in reserve.

There were, as she grew older, a number of disputes, over fashion, friends and scholastic failures, but nothing severe enough to send the Hardings searching for the yellowing sheets of paper, which delineated the particular problems that might be corrected at the source.

"She plays the piano nicely," Mrs. Harding would say, to guests who saw the darting shadow of her nubile figure flitting in and out among the rooms.

"She has a good head on her shoulders," Mr. Harding would say to assorted friends. "She's going to make a damned fine accountant someday."

But the ripening Missy became as sheer and fleeting as a shadow on the lawn. They could not catch her. From dawn to dusk she fled them, always just out of their reach. It was only late at night or early in the morning, when they stole into her room, that they caught a glimpse of the perfect robot baby they had bought, still glowing with a soft light and an innocence of face, as if she had never been used yet.

Perhaps it hasn't been so bad, after all, Mrs. Harding would think.

Maybe it's been better than I thought, Mr. Harding would muse, while adding numbers in his head — room, board, clothing, education — and counting them against the obvious rewards in momentary happiness. Maybe it all comes out even in the end.

The strangest, most unexpected things happened to her. Her dark hair turned almost to gold, a shimmering, frosty gold, and her sea-blue eyes deepened to a vivid forest green. It was unaccountable, except by some accident of chemistry or misapplied science dabbling in the affairs of sacrosanct humanity.

"She isn't exactly what we ordered, you'll have to admit," Mrs. Harding would say while watching the elusive Missy breeze past her with whistling skirts.

"No, she isn't," Mr. Harding would sigh. "But she's been good." He would gaze in the distance, like a sailor recalling lost, uncharted islands.

Her complex machinery clicked and tapped and wound her into full bloom, until she was an enchantress, flinging back her golden hair and leaving her warm breath on everything she touched. They could sniff her moist, pubescent odor in the furniture and in the darkening rooms at night, especially at night, when her absence lay on the house like a thick and palpable mist.

"Isn't she *home* yet?" Mr. Harding would demand in a petulant voice. "Where have you been and what have you been doing?" he would growl when her slight form rustled through the door at last.

"I've been out, I've been with friends," she would murmur and then glide past him like a fairy queen in flight.

Sometimes when she was eluding him this way, he thought he saw a strange metallic gleam in her eyes, and he thought he heard a frantic thumping, much like, if she had been human, the sound of a wildly beating heart.

"Well," Mrs. Harding would mutter, "I certainly hope the Perfect Robot Baby Company has worked out some of the bugs in their product since we bought ours. False advertising is what it is. Pure and simple. Promise you a perfect baby and all you get is a lifetime of trouble."

"Um, yes," Mr. Harding would agree. He had little to say to either of them anymore. Mostly he questioned everything silently, as if something in his life had gone out of control and left him speechless.

The ultimate rupture came when she was not quite eighteen. To the Hardings, of course, she was still a babe in arms, unfinished and unrefined and as much in need of their enveloping care as when they had first unwrapped her in the nursery.

But Missy had been programmed to think at this stage with all the frenetic agility of real-life children and so held her parents' judgments in little regard.

"I'm quitting school," she announced. "I'm going to New York to be an actress."

116

She twisted a purple scarf into a bow-knot at her neck and flung the tail across her shoulder.

"Oh, my heavens," said Mrs. Harding. She sank to the couch and began to fan herself with her fingers.

"Walter, *do* something," she cried.

"Now look here, young lady," he began, shaking a rigid finger at her, "your mother and I... all these years... no daughter of mine... actress my hind foot...

"Go to your room," he shouted finally, pointing the way with the same finger. "We'll discuss this later."

"*No*, Daddy," stormed Missy. "There's nothing to discuss. I've made up my mind. I'm going to be an actress, a *great* actress!" She spoke in a dramatic, lilting voice, with her eyes raised toward the heavens.

"Walter, *do* something," Mrs. Harding said again.

"There's nothing he *can* do, Mother," said Missy. "I've got my *own* life to live, apart from this dreary middle-class trap *you* are in, and there's nothing you can do to stop me. I'll be famous someday, you wait and see." When she spoke, her face seemed to be swimming in a luminous, blue-green sea. Click, click, click and tap, tap, tap, they thought they heard, the buzz and hum and murmur of maladjusted parts setting their hearts on fire this way. What else could it be?

"Mildred, where is the warranty?" Mr.

117

Harding said. "It's time we got this settled once and for all."

"You didn't bring her back any too soon," Manager said in a mellowed voice. "Your warranty runs out in two months. After that the programming would go into an unalterable phase, determining, with slight variations due to atmosphere and ambient conditions, the life mode and characteristics of the machine for the remainder of its operational duration. Some sixty-five years, in accordance with the accepted, tested standard. The standard standard, you might say.

"What seems to be the trouble this time? Of more consequence than the other two occasions, I hope."

"Well," said Mr. Harding, rising to his full height, "we feel that it is time you made good on your promise to us, enacted some eighteen years ago."

Mrs. Harding nodded from the depths of the cracking vinyl couch.

"Which was what?" said Manager.

"Which *was*," said Mr. Harding, "that we were buying a perfect robot baby which would develop into a perfect robot child, just as you advertised."

"I see," said Manager and began to laugh, an odd, clucking laugh. "And did you think that you were buying a baby which would be a perfect robot, or did you think that you were buying a robot that would be a perfect duplicate of a real-life child?"

"Well, I suppose," said Mr. Harding,

118

"that we wanted something as much like the real thing as possible, since we couldn't have the real thing ourselves."

"Yes, yes," chimed in Mrs. Harding, "as much like the real thing as possible."

"And what is your complaint, then, about the Perfect Robot Baby?" asked Manager, staring impatiently into a clock implanted in the wall.

"She has been destructive," said Mrs. Harding eagerly.

"And disobedient," added Mr. Harding.

"And rebellious," said Mrs. Harding. "And she insists on wearing strange, wild clothes."

"And on keeping company with misfits," said Mr. Harding.

"And she won't do what we say," said Mrs. Harding.

"Or become what we want her to become," said Mr. Harding.

"Not to mention the fact that she wants to be an *actress*, of all things," said Mrs. Harding with her last ounce of breath.

"And I suppose," said Manager, leaning wearily against an ancient desk, "that she has caused you countless sleepless nights... and endless days of tedious concern... and moments of suspense too dire to bear..."

"Yes, yes, precisely," the Hardings said in chorus, greedily devouring this affirmation of their grief.

"...and that she has sapped your physical vitality," went on Manager, "and depleted your material resources to an alarming extent..."

119

"Yes, yes, to an alarming extent," put in Mr. Harding. "She's never been denied a thing that money could buy."

"...and intruded upon your privacy... and robbed you of the time and energy to reach your goals..."

"Indeed, she has," said Mrs. Harding in a strident voice.

"...and caused you to look sometimes in wonder at her, marveling at the curious imperfection of her beauty, which only you could admire... and filled you with a painful longing to imbue her with all your knowledge and experience..."

"Yes, we've done that," said Mr. Harding in a low voice. "We've done that."

"And I suppose," said Manager, with a deep, soul-weary sigh, "that she has occasioned, deliberately, of course, those moments when your fondest wish was to draw her to your bosom and console her, or merely hold her, fending off the threat of threatening life..."

"Mildred," murmured Mr. Harding, reaching for his wife's hand.

"...and those times," Manager continued, "when this beastly contraption called a child has caused you to wake in the night and go gaze upon her, throbbing with an awareness of her vulnerability, her utter transparency."

Manager stood up full height, eyes glowing fiercely.

"For she can be destroyed, you know, if you desire. I can have her dismantled and recycled, as easily as I dashed the model

120

baby on the wall, when you first came to me."

"*No,*" cried out the Hardings, jumping to their feet. "Not Missy!"

"Oh, well," sighed Manager, slumping over the desk. "It's just as well. We're overstocked anyway. There's nowhere near the demand for babies that there was before."

"Mildred," said Mr. Harding, his eyes melting to a soft gaze, "perhaps..."

"Perhaps, Walter," echoed Mrs. Harding, "perhaps we should go home."

She took the yellow papers from her purse, crumpled them in her hand, let the brittle particles float to the floor and together they left the store.

*Originally published in the August 1977 issue of *Woman's Day Magazine.*

8 <u>MR. FINLAY'S GRANDIOSE ILLUSION</u>

"Well, where were you off to *last* night?" asked Mrs. Finlay sarcastically. "To Timbuktu?"

Some not-so-gentle soul, listening, might have thought it served her right that a large glob of orange marmalade slipped from her knife and into her lap just then.

"Oh, Hilda, it was *marvelous*," exuded Mr. Finlay, his face beaming through the bluish shadow of his morning whiskers. "Victoria Falls, this time. Just imagine, Hilda, *Victoria Falls*. If only you could have been there with me. But then, of course, you *were* there, weren't you, and just didn't know it.

"Would you mind passing the orange marmalade, dear?" he asked mildly.

"There isn't any left," she said, scooping the fallen globule from her lap and spreading it onto her toast with a forefinger.

"Why, I do believe it was the most spectacular sight I've seen yet," said Mr. Finlay, biting into a piece of dry toast. "Even more so than the Great Pyramid of Cheops, which is something I never thought I'd hear myself say. I looked down and there was this great white wall of water, rushing, careening, diving, thundering, downward and downward to some bottomless, unknown place.

And even from our great height I could hear the magnificent roar of it, like a Beethoven symphony, crashing and bellowing."

"Lester, you're crazy," said Mrs. Finlay, simply. If there was one thing which could be said of Hilda Finlay, it was that she always got right to the heart of things; no beating around the bush for *her*.

It was just this trait, in fact, which had first attracted Mr. Finlay to his future bride. They had been introduced to each other at the wake of a mutual friend, during a period when Mr. Finlay was unemployed, and two days later Hilda Renfro-soon-to-be-Finlay had secured for him a position as envelope stuffer for Parson's Mail Order and Genuine License Plate, Inc., an occupation he pursued to this day, and three days after their auspicious meeting, she had him standing, awestruck, before a judge in the county court house, possessed of two five-dollar gold wedding bands and a marriage certificate. Together they had sailed the sea of matrimony ever since, some twenty-three years now, their matrimonial ship heaving, more often than not, in her direction, but still, plotting its course over mostly calm waters.

Until recently, that is.

"And I'll tell you another thing," she said, hoisting a forkful of scrambled egg, "if you keep *up* this craziness, I'm going to take you — drag you, if I have to - directly to a doctor, a head headshrinker, even though we can't afford it, God knows."

"But, Hilda, darling," said Mr. Finlay, bewildered, "it's not a question of my *keeping it up*. It just happens — I don't know how - but it just *happens*. If only you'd stay up with me some night, as I've begged you to. Why, you've missed some of the most glorious sights already, the Acropolis, and Mont St. Michel, and ..."

"Lester, shut up and eat your oatmeal," she commanded, flicking an errant crumb from his collar.

"I'm so sorry to have kept you waiting," said Dr. Oppenheimer, settling into his leather-cushioned chair with a deep, weary sigh which seemed to rise, all the way from his toes.

"Lots of crazy people running around these days, huh, doc?" inquired Hilda Finlay.

He made no reply, but his steely-blue eyes turned the least bit dull, and he stopped himself, in the middle of another great sigh, as if he were afraid of hyperventilating.

They were sitting around a low, circular table, a heavy oak table which was marvelously carved out into a little bowl in the center. Magazines and pamphlets of all sizes and shapes had been thrown carelessly, or so it seemed, into the carved-out bowl. There were a couple of humor magazines and a gaily decorated children's book, entitled *Parents Can Be Pests*, but mostly they were slick covered publications advertising articles, such as "Depression: The Pros and Cons," and "Schizophrenia in the Suburbs, a Growing Phenomenon."

Lester Finlay leaned forward in his chair, craning his neck painfully as he pretended to leaf through one of the more formidable-looking pamphlets. For he was very nervous and uncomfortable. It wasn't at all as he had expected it to be.

He'd had it in the back of his mind, ever since Hilda told him about the appointment, that he would be led into the room, alone, to lie upon a soft, curving couch and tell a kindly doctor about his adventures. But it wasn't turning out that way in the least. First of all, Hilda had made him dress up in his best suit and tie, just as if they were going to see the preacher, instead of a "Head Headshrinker", as she put it. And then there was the business of her being in the room with him. He certainly hadn't counted on that, for he knew how she felt about his "adventures", and it was bad enough, lately, just to try to tell about them in the privacy of their home, much less in front of a stranger.

Dr. Oppenheimer leaned back in his chair and clasped his hands together, looking suddenly more relaxed.

"Now then, Mr. Finlay," he said after clearing his throat loudly, "when did you first have the idea that your house... uh... that your house... *flies*?"

"Isn't that the craziest thing you ever

heard?" said Hilda, scooting up to the edge of their seat, excitedly.

"Please, Mrs. Finlay," said Dr. Oppenheimer, casting his cool, anesthetizing gaze upon her. "The fact is, what seems, shall we say, *extraordinary* to one person is a mere fact of the mundane world to the next.

"As I was saying," he proceeded, "when were you first... er... *under the impression* that your house *flies*, Mr. Finlay?"

Mr. Finlay jerked at his tie - which he wore, like a boa constrictor, about his neck - and fidgeted in his seat.

"Really, Mr. Finlay," soothed the doctor, "you needn't be the least bit nervous. We are all friends here, and you may say anything, *anything* at *all*," and he darted a quick warning glance at Hilda, who then slouched back in her chair, pouting.

"Well," began Mr. Finlay, surprised at the sound of his own voice, "it all started about three months ago - three months ago, was it, Hilda…?"

"Two months and eighteen days," she said, refusing to look up from her lap.

"...when I was sleeping just as sound as you please," he continued, his voice growing stronger with each word. "And then, when it was about, oh, 1:15, 1:18 maybe, in the a.m., I woke up with this terrible thirst. That happens to me sometimes when we've had fried food for dinner. Not that I'm complaining, though, mind you. No one makes fried fish or hash browns better than Hilda."

"Please, go on with the story, Mr. Finlay," interrupted the doctor, beginning to sigh again.

"Well, as I was saying, I had this terrible thirst, and I got out of bed to go to the kitchen for a drink of water, and all the way there I had this peculiar feeling that the floor was... you know... kind of swaying underneath my feet. But I didn't pay too much attention to it, thought I was still just... you know... half asleep or something. But when I got to the kitchen, and opened the cabinet to get a glass, seemed as though the cabinet kind of leaned away from me, like the house was tilting to one side, the way a boat does."

"Yes, yes, go on," said Dr. Oppenheimer. His eyes had lost their dull cast, and indeed, were beginning to take on glinty sheen.

"Well, I managed to get the glass of water somehow and was about halfway down the hallway when I felt this jolt. I think we must have hit an air pocket just then — like in an airplane, you know, when the thing seems to give a little belch and go out of control for a moment - because there was this big bump, and everything tilted to one side, for sure. I fell against the wall, just barely managing to stay on my two feet, and the water splashed all over my pajamas, the blue rayon ones that Hilda got me for my birthday. It was only the second time I'd ever had them on."

Mr. Finlay paused for breath, during

which fleeting moment he noticed that Dr. Oppenheimer had closed his eyes in a sort of painful grimace.

"But I swear to you, doctor," he resumed, refreshed and exhilarated, "that I *still* wouldn't have paid too much attention to it if it hadn't been for this powerful feeling that we were swaying, that we were lifted up somehow and swaying about in the air. And besides, there was this whooshing sound, like air being traveled through at great speed, and yet I remembered that when I had gone to bed that night - about 9:30, 9:45, I think it was — the air outside had been as dead and still as a mummy's breath. Well, I had this irresistible urge to run to one of the windows or the door and look out. And all the way there, to the front door, I sort of had this feeling that I knew what I'd find when I did look out. And sure enough, do you know what I saw when I opened the front door?"

Dr. Oppenheimer opened his eyes wide, as if he had been startled awake.

"No, what?"

"Nothing!" said Mr. Finlay. He stretched back in his chair and stared the doctor square in the face. "I mean nothing but black space - no street lights or parked cars or cats' eyes or any of the things you see when you look outside on a dark night. Just black space for a minute. And then, after I'd blinked my eyes a few times, I started seeing clouds, very dim and filmy, but there they were all right, floating right over the roof and through the patio.

128

Why, I could have reached right out and touched one, if you could do such a thing, which, of course, you can't, their being nothing but milky-colored air. And then I had to take a deep breath and hold on real tight to the door ledge - steeling myself, you might say, in order to look down. Because, once again, I had a feeling that I knew what I'd find when I did. And do you know what it was?"

"Nothing?" asked Dr. Oppenheimer, in a voice which might have seemed, to a practiced ear, to have a slight, ironic edge to it.

"Oh, goodness gracious, no!" cried Mr. Finlay. "Why, it was the most remarkable thing you ever saw. Why, I hardly know how to tell you about it," he gasped. "For there, down below — very, *very* far below — was the middle of the Pacific Ocean, the moonlight just barely illuminating a crashing herd of waves around a tiny island, just a bare speck of land, in the midst of this great silver expanse of water. And when I looked closer, straining my eyes and fighting back a bad case of vertigo, I saw these strange, oddly shaped monoliths, rising out of the ground on that pathetic little piece of land in the middle of the sea. We were moving very fast, of course, we passed over it in the time it takes to snap your fingers, but, still, I knew what it was. I'd seen it a dozen times in magazines, in the *National Geographic*. It was..."

"Easter Island?" asked Dr. Oppenheimer

somewhat flatly. He had taken out a pencil and begun doodling on a long, narrow pad of paper.

"Why, yes," exclaimed Mr. Finlay. "Exactly. Easter Island."

"Hogwash," said Hilda, suddenly stirring in her seat, where she had been sitting languidly, engaged in pushing back the cuticle of her right thumbnail.

"Mrs. Finlay," said Dr. Oppenheimer in a controlled voice, "I feel I must caution you against any further such unwarranted remarks during the remainder of our session, which..." and he glanced meaningfully at his watch here "...is almost over, I fear.

"Just one more question, Mr. Finlay," said the doctor, looking up sad-eyed from his Oyster Rolex, "have you been to other places? I mean… that is... has your house continued to... er... fly through the night?"

"Oh, doctor," breathed Mr. Finlay softly, "if I could but tell you of the wonders I have seen, the crowning achievements of our Mother Nature. Kilimanjaro and K2 and the Great Barrier Reef and the Great Wall and... and..."

"I think we'll be able to see you next week at this same hour," said Dr. Oppenheimer, rising from the depths of his chair in time to a great and final sigh.

"Hogwash," whispered Hilda, in defiance of her warning.

They went three more times to the office of the renowned Dr. Oppenheimer, and on each occasion, Mr. Finlay described his nocturnal journeys into the far beyond aboard his incredible flying house.

They sped, in a manner of speaking, over Mt. Rainier and the Gobi Desert and Tierra del Fuego and the Galapagos Islands and even, chillingly, the Arctic Circle.

"Oh, I do wish you could have been with us, Doctor," said Mr. Finlay graciously, "when we passed over the Cape of Wrath, at the very tip-top of Scotland, you know. The place is so aptly named. Such a fury of angry, tumultuous waves beating themselves to death against the obstinate cliffs. And then there was Stonehenge, so mysterious and enigmatic, and the Matterhorn, oh, that majestic, snow-clad mountain, and Ireland, like a pinch of throbbing greenness dropped accidentally into the sea and..."

"Yes, yes," said the good doctor, chewing absentmindedly on the end of his pencil. "But the point is that you are under the illusion... I mean, it seems to you, Mr. Finlay, that your house is *flying*, taking off, as it were, on these midnight journeys, is that correct?"

"Oh, indeed It does," replied Mr. Finlay. "A marvelous house, a miraculous house, wouldn't you say? Why, it flies so gently, and steadily, that even the queasiest stomach would be hard put to complain.

"My only regret," he said, hurtling downward from the airy heights of his remembered journeys, "is that Hilda will not partake of this wondrous adventure.

"Why, she sleeps like a log through the night, never knowing where she's going, or where she's been. And when she awakes in the morning and I try to tell her of the sun-kissed, ice-bound places we have visited through the night, she merely yawns and nags at me to finish breakfast and dressing in time to get to Parson's Mail Order and Genuine License Plate Company, in order to punch in by 8:00.

"Why, I could never afford to take her to these places on my own," he said, "and now that we have this marvelous flying house she won't go. At least, she won't *realize* her going."

"Hog-waah-"

"Ah-hum-mm, *Mrs*. Finlay," said Dr. Oppenheimer, squeezing the bridge of his Romanesque nose between a thumb and forefinger, "if I could but speak to you in private a moment."

Mr. Finlay was ushered into the garden-like reception room, and as he felt the vinyl-covered, sound-proof door wafting shut behind him, he was stung with a pang of sympathy for his poor, dear wife, Hilda, for he feared that she was about to be reprimanded at last by Dr. Oppenheimer for interjecting, at frequent intervals, her rude and rather coarse remarks into their otherwise sublime discussions.

But that was not the case at all, however. For he - Dr. Oppenheimer - merely wished to reveal to Mrs. Finlay that he had formulated what he thought might be a most expeditious method of showing up her husband's illusions to him as just that – illusions. "You see, Mrs. Finlay, the problem is," said the doctor, circling his desk like a graceful, stalking tiger, "...the problem is that your husband has not yet endeavored to share this delusion of the flying house, with any other person."

"Bet your boots, he *has*," said Mrs. Finlay indignantly. "Why, he's forever after me to stay up with him into the wee, small hours, waiting for the great take-off. Honestly, these men have always got *some* reason not to let a woman get her sleep at night."

"Well, that may very well be the case," said Dr. Oppenheimer, and he slumped into his chair on the next trip round. "But you see, you have not so far succumbed to your husband's pleas to join him on his midnight raids... er, rides. And, therefore, there has been no one present – no *rational* person present – to point out to him that it is merely a grandiose illusion that his house is flying through the night air."

"Aha, I think I see what you mean," said Hilda, as if a light had been switched on in the dusky corridors of her brain. "In other words, if I'm there with him, wide awake, when he starts thinking that the house is taking off again, then I can show him that it's not, that it's still on good, old solid ground. And then he would be cured?"

"Hopefully. If not," sighed the doctor, "I can only suggest that he be institutionalized. And, as a matter of conscience, I just happen to own part interest in a lovely and immaculately landscaped sanitarium on the outskirts of town."

"But if you put him in there," remarked Hilda, in a rare show of speculative foresight, "wouldn't he just think every night that that whole sani-... sani-... - that the whole nut house was flying?"

"Perhaps," replied the weary healer, "but at least *there,* he would have many willing and eager companions, on his extraterrestrial excursions."

That very afternoon, as they were driving home, Hilda Finlay surprised and overjoyed her husband - completely obliterating from his memory the large and looming figures on the doctor's invoice he had just received - by handing him the good news that she would go riding with him that night.

"Oh, Hilda, darling," he cried, throwing one arm around her and causing the car to barely miss swerving into a station wagon full of Boy Scouts, "you've made me the happiest man in the world. How lucky I am, to have a wonderful flying house, and, now, a loving wife to share it with me. I just hope that we'll go somewhere very special tonight. You would have loved the Sahara," he enthused, "knowing your penchant for hot

134

air. That is, knowing how warm-natured you are and all, is what I mean to say, dear."

It was just going on a quarter past midnight, the Finlays ensconced in the his-or-her swivel rockers in the living room, when Lester Finlay suddenly jumped forward in his seat, which an agitated – some might have said, *maniacal* - look in his eyes. "Whee! Here we go. Hold on, Hilda, darling. Up, up and away, as they say."

Hilda did think she felt a sudden lightheadedness and a tiny rumble in the pit of her stomach, but this, she attributed to the half-dozen cups of coffee she had drunk lately, in order to remain alert through the night.

"Ten... fifteen... twenty thousand... twenty-five thousand feet, I'd say, and still climbing," cried out Mr. Finlay, extending both arms and tilting from side to side in imitation of an airplane.

Hilda held on tightly to both arms of her chair. "I know coffee doesn't agree with me at night," she thought, greatly annoyed with herself for her wanton over-indulgence.

Suddenly Mr. Finlay sprang up from his chair and stood in the middle of the room, leaning precariously from side to side, a look of utter ecstasy painting his masterpiece.

"Lester, sit down and stop acting like a fool," growled Hilda, her eyes rolling and her face taking on a slight greenish tint. "Don't you know what they're going to do to you, if you don't cut out this foolishness? Don't you know they're going to put you

135

away, maybe forever?" She held her throat in her hand and hoped she wasn't going to be sick. Never again, she thought, *never* again was she going to drink coffee, not even in the mornings.

"But, Hilda, dearest, can't you feel it?" gushed Mr. Finlay. "The lovely swaying? The great rush of movement? That exotic feeling of suspension? The drifting? I do believe we're drifting now, slowing down. We must have come to some exciting place. Come to the door and look out. It could be anyplace, the Pyrenees - we haven't been there yet - or darkest Africa or the Arabian Desert..."

He swung open the front door, being careful to support himself against the door frame, and peered out, wide-eyed, into the night.

"Well, I'll be," he exclaimed. "Of all things. I never would have guessed. The *Grand Canyon*. Yessir, the Grand Canyon, just as big as life and more than a mile wide, if you'll excuse the pun. Oh, do come and see it, Hilda. It's simply breathtaking."

Mrs. Finlay pushed herself up from her swivel rocker and staggered toward the front door, though she was sorely determined to swing round and head for the bathroom. But she was determined to carry out the plan devised by Dr. Oppenheimer, to cure her husband once and for all of his addlepated, numb-skull obsession.

"Lester, you jerk," she said, heading right for the front door and through it, "there's nothing out there but the front porch and the sidewalk and the..."

"*Hilda*," screamed Mr. Finlay, reaching out a desperate arm into the darkness, while holding on fiercely with one hand to the door ledge.

"...*stree-eeet*," was all the response from his dear wife, in a tiny, hollow voice, accompanied by a slight swishing sound, like curtains blowing mildly in a breeze, diminishing to nothing, to silence.

"Oh, goodness, gracious," he cried aloud, staring out into the length and breadth and width of space about him. "How exasperatingly stupid of me! Anyone with the good fortune to own a flying house should certainly have his head examined, for not laying in a couple of parachutes."

9 IN LIEU OF FRENCH DOORS

Pale yellow doors - *French* doors, no less, opening, onto a throbbing greenness of garden. And through the panes, beyond the sloping lawn and far away, a luscious wash of blue, which was the ocean. The room, what one could see of it in the photograph, was as perfect as the setting: Choice pieces of French furniture, articulate, sublime, and graceful vases filled with pastel flowers; a painting or two, pastoral landscapes from some other planet; and a sprinkling of gracious artifacts, judiciously arranged.

Perfect! thought Milly. *Perfect!*

She looked at the man in the picture, looked through the perfect room to stare at him, as he stood gazing out the yellow-framed squares of glass in his French doors. And something pinched her inwardly, a tiny nibble where her heart was.

My doors, she almost said, catching the thought somewhere between her breast and throat.

He was not particularly tall or handsome. He was a gently aging man, with a luxury of graying hair and a thick, dark beard which concealed his mouth, the soft and unassuming lips which she had found once, much to her surprise. His eyes were tired, and he stooped somewhat, with one arm thrown lazily about the woman at his side,

138

whose face was almost too serene to be taken seriously.

The words beneath the picture in the magazine said: "Author Steven Mendel and his wife, Gertrude Mendel, enjoying the view from their palatial, oceanfront estate."

"Oh, Gertie," Milly said out loud at last, "that could be *me* standing there."

There was a brisk movement behind her, a tap of heel and hiss of breath, and then the warm, brown head, nuzzling deep in her neck.

"Aha, I've caught you," said Joe, blowing hot breath on her cheek when he spoke. "I hate to tell you this, old girl, but you've been staring at that picture all morning. Are you transfixed?" He unfolded slowly upward, brushing his whiskery face along her cheek, up over her ear and through the wealth of ruffled hair. "If so, then we must *un*-transfix you.

"And I know just the way," he laughed.

She turned to look at him, but the mind behind her eyes was far away, in another room with another man.

"It's just the doors, Joe," she murmured. "You know how I love French doors."

"And so, you shall have them, my sweet," he said, moving with great commotion to the cupboard. (*He is*, she mused, *the only person I know who clicks when he walks*, and she placed an asterisk by the thought.) "French doors, Greek doors, Hungarian doors, whatever your heart desires."

He took a glass from the shelf and made

a concert of pouring lemonade into it. "You just wait, Milly. I'm really onto something now. I'm going to make my dream come true this time."

His blue eyes were full of magic, as always, and something in his face, something very bright and sparkling, bespoke a youthfulness he should have shed years ago. Looking at him, she could never quite frown, even if she couldn't quite smile either.

He stopped in the doorway and toasted her with the glass of lemonade. "I'll get you those French doors, Milly, don't you worry.

"And if you're good," he said, tossing her the punch line as he left, "I may even get you a house to go with it."

She closed her eyes and wished him from the room. And when he was gone, his clicking steps an echo in the hall, she turned back to the picture, stared at the gray-haired man, and shook her head.

"Sure, Joe, sure. You have your dreams, a million ways to make a million bucks."

She had left *her* last dream in a peanut butter jar somewhere, she thought. A chunky, freckled fist tugging at her skirt, she had handed down a plate of sandwiches one day, then turned and screwed the lid on tight, sealing in her last dream, hoping it wouldn't go stale.

And she had left it there in airtight safety, all these years... until today.

The man in the picture! *He* had set it free again. Only it was musty now, and cracked around the edges, like some ancient relic, dug up and dusted off and prized for what it had once been.

She slapped shut the magazine, but her thumb caught on the page at which it had been turned, stayed there, willfully, until she flipped open the book once more. And when she looked down at the picture this time, it seemed that the gray-haired man was gazing, not through his graceful doors to the watery blueness below, but straight at her.

She had known him years ago, before she married Joe, of course, when she was old enough to know her way around and yet still young enough to get lost. They had met at a seaside resort in winter, when everything was frozen gray and lush with silence. Time had seemed suspended in that place, and movement, also, except for the frequent, gusty winds from off the ocean.

The ornate shops were closed, the sidewalks bare; the few, small restaurants still open, resounded with the occasional clatter of a single coffee cup or glass. A ghost town, in other words, but an elegant one. And somehow, behind that austere and silent exterior, one could sense a painful, human throbbing.

"I saved three years to come here," she had told him in a mock-complaint, "and then, dumb luck, my vacation falls in the dead of winter. But where else could you see salt water icicles?"

He had laughed. But he had often laughed at her, in a gentle, prodding way, as though her naïve enthusiasm were strangely alien and entertaining. "Or build a snowman out of sand?" he'd said, and then they both had laughed.

He was not yet famous then, at least not to speak of, or so that she would know. Perhaps in the slightly frosty circles of the literary world, his name was beginning to be spoken in tones of jealousy and admiration and expectancy. But he never mentioned who or what he was, and to Milly he had merely seemed a charming drifter, a man out of place and Time, whose eyes and voice contained a cold, sad ocean of their own.

She had often thought, since that time, that he was surely the loneliest man she had ever known, his loneliness expressed through a deep, quiet pain in his eyes.

And what woman can resist a man who pleads for solace with his gaze?

Lunch! remembered Milly suddenly, starting up from her reverie, *I must get lunch*.

"Might as well be peanut butter sandwiches," she thought, with a wry mental grin, "now that the jar is open."

"The boys and I are going to the beach," said Joe, as she was stacking the luncheon dishes on the counter. "Wanna come along?" He was trailing a beach towel and three dark-haired children in his wake.

Milly didn't answer, but she dropped a plate into the sink with a loud, clanging reverberation. She thought of the hot,

142

stifling beach, and instantly her mind flew away to that other, frozen waterfront.

"Say, sweetheart," said Joe, turning her around with two, strong hands, "why don't you let me take you away from all this?" He was clean-shaven now, and soft, and sweet-smelling, and even in the heat, his warm skin against her own was dangerously compelling.

"Not today, Joe," she said, pulling away. "You go along, without me." She bent down to kiss the moist, summer faces of the children, wiping a lick of peanut butter from the youngest's chin.

"Okay," he said softly. "Looks like you're busy anyway, doing some kind of psychic experiment with that picture in the magazine."

She imagined she saw a flicker of consternation in his eyes, and her only thought, uncharitably, was, "Serves you right, Joe Healey. Wonder a while."

When they were gone, the silence in the house was palpable, almost like a shroud fallen, thought Milly, wincing at her own description. She lay down to take a nap, slipping between the cool sheets with a long sigh of relief.

She switched on a small, electric fan on the bedside table and sank back, tired and heavy, to listen to its soothing drone. But it only brought the memories rushing back once more, against her will, like illuminated pictures in her mind.

He had bought her books, that winter by

143

the sea, novels with strange names and sparse little magazines of poetry. And she had tried to read them all, until her eyes and mind were clouded over with a fine glaze of wonderment and fatigue. So many things she'd never known before, or even dreamed of. So many vivid pictures emerging from the pages. And they had talked, or at least she had listened, in a trance, while Steven Mendel talked, as they sat together in the evenings, drawn closer to one another by the frigid breeze.

"You know, I think it's funny," he had said once, staring at the frosty cliffs on the horizon, "how we tend to read one another in large, bold letters, while we read ourselves in fine print. Which makes it so easy to skip a line here and there." And then he'd laughed, the small, hoarse laugh which seemed to urge her not to take him seriously.

But, of course, she had, tripping on his words as if she were drunk.

Together they had explored the frozen canyons of the ghost town, tight-knit in that peculiar and fiercesome kind of intimacy that only strangers share. With no common past or future to bind them, and no outstanding debts to one another, they had wrung the most from every moment, alive to each nuance of wit or insight or sudden, nameless sorrow.

She discovered, under his benign tutelage, the joys of French cuisine, staring wide-eyed, night after night, at the lava-flow of sauces on her plate, beneath

144

which wonders lay. And they had window-shopped on drowsy afternoons, gazing through the frosted glass of shuttered shops at small, priceless treasures.

One day they found a souvenir stand still doing business by the beach, and he had bought her a sea horse pin, which was made of shell and covered over with a luminous glaze.

"Something for you to remember me by," he'd whispered, pressing it into her hand. It was still buried in a drawer somewhere, among a lifetime's collection of mementos.

Suddenly Milly laughed, struck by a sharp, contrasting memory of the way in which *Joe* had courted her. Then, it had been all hot dogs and beer and baseball games, with Milly picking up the tab, most times. And month-long Sundays with his family, during which she had always seemed to be inching her way through the boisterous, Irish crowd to look for him. And endless nights spent listening to his repertoire of dreams, with a mixture of delirium and alarm. Some small, inner voice had told her even then that he was dangerous, a man who walked on clouds instead of solid ground. But the sparkling blue eyes and tawny skin and quick, effusive laughter sealed her fate, catching her unawares while she was sighing.

Now, all these years later, it was still beer and hot dogs, and dreams snatched out of the sky.

Milly groaned and rolled onto her side, as if to turn away from her thoughts. But they would not be cast off so easily. How many things had she always wanted, lovely, lovely things, that she would never own? And how many places were there in the world that she would never see? And how many small, exquisite moments that she would never experience? It was silly, of course, but she had a recurring vision of herself, dressed in a flowing gown, sweeping through a door into a garden, where people waited, breathless, for her presence. In the fantasy, she was pristine in beauty, standing grandly alone and independent, the way women were in movies.

As it was, she never swept through doors but rather dragged, fettered by armies of tenacious, clinging children.

How did Gertrude Mendel go through doors, she wondered?

On the last evening of her vacation in that far-off year, which she remembered as though it were a fairy-tale, told in her childhood, she and Steven Mendel had walked along the beach at sunset, hardly speaking to each other, holding hands. Now and then he squeezed her fingers gently, which she understood as a message of regret.

When a blue-gray darkness fell, she stooped and pointed to the sky. "There, just above us, the Milky Way. You know," she'd murmured, gazing at the milky whiteness in the sky, "I'll never understand how we can stand apart and look up, from such a distance, at something we're a part of."

"What?" he asked, suddenly grasping her by both arms.

"I said, I'll never understand..." she began and never finished, for he had bent to kiss her.

And hadn't he... hadn't he given her a sea shell that night, with their names inscribed on the silky, inner surface with a pebble? She had a vague recollection of his tossing it into the sea, and of watching it wash away on the waves.

Maybe he had, and maybe she had dreamed it, for everything about that time was so far off and gauzy now, like looking at a landscape through a veil.

She had never seen him after that, and she had never heard from him. Years later, while reading a magazine in the Maternity Ward, she was astounded to see his name on a book review. And there had been numerous other articles, and sharp, sniping chatter at cocktail parties, until his name had joined the proverbial list of household words. Once she saw him listed on the credits for a movie and had a sudden urge for popcorn.

But for the most part, he had faded in her consciousness. Time and Life and harsh reality had driven him into the distant regions of dim memory. For theirs had been a brief encounter, after all; they had touched each other's hearts and minds with all the grace of floating feathers, barely a tickle in the long, hard scheme of things.

She hadn't realized until today, seeing his picture in the magazine, how deep a wound a feather could inflict.

It was too hot to sleep, as though she could be blessed with such a sweet, obliterating gift, anyway, and so she rose, with the weight of ages on her shoulders, and tried to think of dinner. Peanut Butter Supreme? *Coc au* Peanut Butter? Or, perhaps, fresh peanut butter on the half-shell? No, no. This was Real Life, and miracles could not be gotten from a jar.

Joe and the children slid into the house on a fine film of grit and sand, with small, translucent drops of moisture on their cheeks, still carrying the sun in their hair and smiles. She transported soggy clothing to the laundry room and dropped it, with a grimace, into the washer. Then she mopped the little pools of wetness from the floor and patted sun-burned arms and listened, crooning, to the tales of high adventure on the beach. There was the customary cut-foot to be tended to, with much ado, and one, predictable belly-ache, from too much Coke and cotton candy. At one point, sinking back with laughter, she wailed, "Wait! Wait! You're telling me too much at once," then reached out and lifted up her child and hugged him fiercely.

She had disposed of the magazine, not

148

actually thrown it away but hidden it beneath a stack of papers on the porch. Any time before tomorrow morning, when the garbage collectors would come to carry off the refuse of their lives indiscriminately, she could retrieve it. If she wanted to.

Not that it was necessary anymore really, for the picture was burned, indelibly, on her brain, and the only question – a moot one - was whether it gave her more pleasure than pain.

Dinner, as it turned out, was frankfurters and beans, to no one's great surprise. The children lifted their forks and spoons up, as if they were heavy chains, and halfway through the meal, their breathing grew hoarse, their eyelids fluttered, and they leaned against the table for support.

"Oh, dear, oh, dear," thought Milly, with an inward groan, looking at them, "how can they be such devils in the morning and such angels at night?"

Joe was merely silent during dinner, and let his beer grow warm. "You know, Milly," he said, when they had tucked the children into bed, "I'm thinking maybe you need a vacation from us."

"From who?" she asked obstinately, without looking up from her book.

"You know. The kids and me." His voice was hoarse and low; he sounded tired. "I mean, I know it isn't easy for you, being stuck in the house all day, with all you have to do. And maybe we – the kids and me –

are not enough. Maybe there's something else you ought to get out of life."

She couldn't bring herself to look at him.

"Don't be silly, Joe," she said, regretting the harshness of her tone. "I'm perfectly content."

She hoped he hadn't noticed the catch in her voice, or the way her eyes squeezed shut, when she had spoken.

"I'm not so sure about that," he murmured, turning away.

Oh, God, there was that look again, of melting helplessness and yearning, drawn like a picture on his face; his eyes grown dim, like bright lights suddenly extinguished, and the merest quiver of uncertainty playing on his lips.

At this moment he looked very much like one of her children, exquisitely vulnerable, which was so unfair.

In some perverse reaction, she snapped shut her book and growled at him, "Oh, Joe, go to bed. You're letting your fancies run away with you again."

She felt almost like an interloper, or a refugee from the enemy camp, when she crawled into bed beside him after midnight. He had thrown back the covers, because of the heat, and she had to nudge his long, lean body sideward, in order to make room. "He even sleeps like a child," she thought, "with his mouth half open and his eyelids flickering with dreams."

Her head fell against something hard

beneath the pillow, with a slight, crunching sound. She reached behind and extracted a small, brown box, an empty carton from the hardware store. "Oh, Lord," was her first thought, "no one puts anything away but me."

Only it *wasn't* empty. For something thumped inside it, some tiny, solid thing, some minor treasure secreted in the soft recesses of her bed.

She carried it into the kitchen and switched on a light. There was a note inside, in Joe's scrawling handwriting, which said: "In lieu of French doors, this is all I have to give you, besides my heart." And under that, upon a bed of cotton, lay a large, fluted sea shell, a gloriously curving, luminescent thing, on the underside of which was scratched the message, "I love you, Milly."

So, she hadn't dreamed it, after all. But she had painted someone else in Joe's bright colors, had given someone else his warmth and tenderness. "Of course," she whispered, with a tingle of revived remembrance, "that night we had the picnic on the beach..."

She waited a while in silence, thinking hard, then stepped onto the porch and, digging beneath the stack of discarded papers, pulled out the magazine and tossed it, with a thud, into the garbage can. Then she tip-toed through the darkness back to bed once more and eased her body next to his.

In a moment she rose up and, turning to bend over him, she kissed his salty cheek.

"What was *that* for?" he grumbled in a drowsy voice, stirring underneath her.

Milly smiled and, bending low again, she whispered, "In lieu of French doors, my darling."

10 <u>WHEN THE TIME IS RIGHT</u>*

It's only the middle of April and the lawn is still covered with a fine film of dewy moisture from the last shower, so that it looks as though a treasure of tiny jewels had been sprinkled on the grass. A tepid breeze whispers through the slit of open window in the kitchen, and the sun appears on whim throughout the day. It is, in other words, that lazy and becalming period of suspension between seasons.

So, naturally, when Christopher came to me this morning and asked if we could have a picnic lunch in the yard instead of the usual snatched sandwich at the breakfast counter, I immediately said, "Not today. We'll do it later, when the time is right," my mind leaping forward automatically to some more auspicious moment in the future. I might have been an actor in a play, speaking my lines on cue, so easily did the words spring from my lips. And they brought the ageless response from four-year-old Christopher; his idea squelched, his hopes smothered, the bright sparkle of his eyes turned instantly to leaden dullness, as though a door had been slammed shut in his face.

How well I remember.

When the time is right. It was a phrase my mother used, and her mother before her, and no doubt her mother before her, through a long line of people who, for some reason lost in the past, had learned to live in a perpetual state of postponement, waiting for "right times." The right time to fall in love, or to marry, or to have a child. The right time to take a detour through the park on the way home, or to have a talk, or to see a bird's nest in a tree. So that all that remained of daily life was an endless preparation for and anticipation of things to come, when the time would be right. From generation to generation, the phrase and the philosophy have been handed down like family heirlooms, and I, apparently, am the current keeper.

As I watched Christopher's small, sad figure in departure, I was cast back in memory to that first occasion when those words first made their mark on my mind.

How many times did I hear my grandmother tell the story of her first true love? She was very old by then, of course, and eager to make her life an open book before it closed. My grandfather – that stern autocrat of our family whom I remember only as a blurred image of clenched jaw and steely gaze – was dead, and Gran'ma had left her small New England village to come and live with us in Boston. From the moment she first stepped across the threshold with her ancient, musty bags and parcels, she seemed to fade more and more each day until she was almost transparent, a phantom who flitted through the house leaving a scent of lavender on everything she touched. I never knew when I would round a corner and find her whispering and beckoning to me to follow her into her room. "Come, child. Come in and let me tell you a story," she'd hiss, as though we were conspirators.

It frightened me at first to follow this otherworldly wisp of woman into the dim sanctuary of her room; it was permeated with the scent of lavender sachet and old age. But then she would coax me onto the quilted mountain of her bed and begin to tell the story in a hoarse but vibrant whisper, her fingers fluttering like ten butterflies as she spoke. And before I could find my voice to plead for release, I would be lost in the forest of her words.

The story was always the same, of her romance with Bobby McPhail. "My bonnie Bob," she called him, her childhood sweetheart. Bobby was a blue-eyed blond with an ample quota of freckles and enough mischief for three leprechauns. He'd come to call for her on Sunday afternoons for a walk along the pier, and he always brought a present. Once it was a five-pound box of penny lollipops, which took her a year to lick into oblivion, she said. Another time it was a shimmering feather from a peacock, and she didn't dare ask him how he got it. "He'll never miss it, the way he's decked out," Bobby had said, by way of forestalling the question. And most of all, she loved to tell me about the day when Bobby appeared on her doorstep with an enormous, shiny box, proclaiming that he had brought her a gift that no one else in the world could give her. She opened the box to find it stuffed with butcher paper and old newsprint and was in the midst of giving him a harsh lecture on his antics immaturity when she discovered, lying there on the bottom of the box, a slender lock of Bobby's fair hair, tired round with a blue ribbon.

Ah, the excessive subtlety of young love!

My grandfather didn't approve of Bobby McPhail, of course, which only made the story better. It's easy to imagine this stalwart Victorian eminence standing with thrust finger, his coattails flying in the breeze stirred by his righteous fury, as he orders the elfin Bobby from the premises. And all to the tune of Gran'ma's heartsick wailing. But Bobby wasn't one to take an edict seriously, especially if it came between himself and what he wanted. And one night, shortly after he had been banished and banned for the umpteenth time, Gran'ma was sitting alone in the parlor, playing Chopin's *Minute Waltz*, when she thought she heard a strange, scratchy noise. The wind rattling the windows, perhaps, or a mouse in the attic. But then she felt a thrilling presence in the room, both frightening and fascinating, drawing nearer and nearer (these are Gran'ma's own words).

She didn't dare to turn around but kept on playing, and just as she reached the frenzied conclusion of the piece, there was a stunning movement behind her and her thick, brown hair cascaded down her back.

156

Bobby had stolen in on his light feet and pulled the clasp from her hair. Before she could cry out, he gave the swivel stool a push and she was twirled around to find herself caught in his embrace. He kissed her once – passionately, she said – before darting into the darkness once more and was not heard from again for many weeks. Even Bobby McPhail, one imagines, knew when he had overreached himself.

Whenever she told me this story, which was often, I would feel an inexplicable shiver run through me as she came to the part where her hair came down; indeed, I *still* shiver to recall it.

Bobby, frankly, always sounded like quite a catch to me, in spite of great-grandfather's more practical assessment. I had, in fact, drawn a pretty-thorough picture of him in my mind from Gran'ma's oft repeated stories. I never imagined him as being very handsome – people of such great, good spirit usually aren't – but when I closed my eyes, I felt I could actually see his broad, infectious smile and that twinkle of budding mischief in his eyes. In spite of myself, and with a twinge of guilt, I wondered how she could have settled for dour Grandpa after the giddy delights of "Bonny Bob."

But the answer to that was at the end of her story. "It was always understood, of course, that Bobby and I would marry, when the time was right," she'd add as epilogue.

157

They had neatly plotted out their lives, it seems, on those ambling walks along the pier on Sunday afternoons. Bobby would be a carpenter and she a seamstress, and someday he would build their own white house for them at the end of Linden Street. And in a few years, the rafters would be trembling from the sounds of little Bobbies and Annettes, all freckle-faced and fair and full of mischief. (One does shudder slightly to think of it.) And life from then on, even with its inevitable sprinkling of trial and sorrow, would be like a gift in a shiny box.

Only that "right time" never came. For Bobby skipped off to war in 1917 (I can't really think of him *marching*) and he never returned, leaving Gran'ma with a peacock feather and a lock of hair and a dream of a white house to hold on to. And all the rest was relegated to that cruel realm of might-have-been.

At this point in the story, she would look, into the distance, and speak softly, as though asking a question of the air, "I forget now what it was we were waiting for."

The story always thrilled and horrified me. A hundred times I wanted to cry out, "Why? Why didn't you marry Bobby and have babies and live happily ever after at the end of Linden Street?" But one didn't question the mysterious motives of grown-ups, who seemed to do everything in life but what would make them happy.

One day I rushed into the house after school, eager to hear the story yet another time, and found the door to Gran'ma's room was open and the room empty. Her small, gilt-edged Bible was missing from the bedside table and her pink flannel gown was thrown across the end of the unmade bed. And all was silence in the house.

Something awful had happened, I knew, and for some reason I thought of Bobby McPhail, so alive that one could hardly think of him ever being dead, and yet he was, buried in a field in France. And a cold chill ran through me to think that if it could happen to Bobby it could happen to anyone, even Gran'ma.

My mother came home very late that night and dragged herself into my room, walking almost like a ghost with chains. She sat on the edge of the bed and stared at me through large, hollow, unseeing eyes.

"Where's Gran'ma?" I demanded, as though my own mother had abducted her and carried her off to some lurid imprisonment.

"She's very ill," my mother answered in a toneless voice. "She's in the hospital. We'll have to wait and see."

"I want to see her!" I cried out, full of a presentiment of doom.

"Yes, yes, I'll take you to see her," she said, "when the time is right."

The house seemed intolerably empty after that. The door to Gran'ma's room was kept shut, as though she were still there, weaving tales of her own Bobby McPhail.

Through unconquerable habit, I would

159

rush to that room each afternoon, hoping, through some miracle, to find her sitting up in bed with her multicolored threads and fabrics spread out across the quilt, the clacking needles abruptly ceasing upon my arrival. And each time I turned a corner in the house, I'd expect to find her small, bent, airy figure beckoning to me to follow her into the room for yet another story or, better yet, the old, familiar one.

Each night when my mother came home, ragged and weary, I would put the same command to her. "I want to see Gran'ma. You must take me to see her, before it's too late."

"Yes, yes, child," she'd say. "I'll take you to see her, when the time is right."

But she never did, and Gran'ma, like "Bonny Bob," never came home again. And I never got to tell her that I understood. That I understood about Bobby McPhail and love and hope and spirit. That I understood that life was *meant* to be full of moments of joy. And most of all, I never got to tell her that I understood how sorry she was that *she* had understood it all too late.

And now another phrase is gently humming in my mind, a bit of poetry my own dear Charlie used to prod me with when we were young:

"*Gather ye rosebuds while ye may,*
Old Time is still a-flying."

160

But I really must pull the curtain on these reveries, for it's almost noon and the sun has elected to shine again, however briefly.

I must make some sandwiches and boil some eggs and find some ancient rag of tablecloth to soak up the moisture on the lawn. Then I must find where Christopher is hiding and tell him that the right time is now.

*Originally published in the May 1979 issue of *Ladies' Home Journal Magazine.*

11 <u>THE MANDALA LIZARD</u>

Salamandorff was an old-world lizard, long and lean and slippery. "I survived the Holocaust," he liked to say, while the fires still leapt and crackled in his eyes.

He had a vague reputation as a minor luminary in the scientific world, though his work was often wildly esoteric and misunderstood – even, at times, resented and denounced, for reasons a layman would have shuddered to comprehend. There were also dark rumors of some nameless "trouble" in his past, some lurid scandal which the years had camouflaged. These were enhanced, no doubt, by his primitive appearance and his odd, lurking manner.

Laura sent up an alarm about him almost immediately after he came to work at the laboratory with her and Dr. Dinir. She had only to look at him once and have him look back, leering, through his moist and flickering eyes, to feel her heart sink with dread.

"There's something terribly wrong about him," she whispered, standing behind Dinir as he sat crouching over a vial which boiled and bubbled like a witch's brew. "He reminds me of a lizard," she said, "and not just because of his name, either."

"What, then?" asked Dinir, squinting into his microscope. His display of *blasé* inattention was an act, a shield against her piercing presence.

"There's something positively... *primeval* about the man," she said, groping to express her horror. "Not to mention that he's always filthy," she added, as though feeling the need of some more material complaint. "How can a reputable scientist work with dirty fingernails, for god's sake?" A storm was raging in her sea-green eyes and her hands twitched nervously in the pockets of her long smock.

"But, ah, there you have a flaw in your analogy," said Dinir, as he whirled around to face her. "For lizards, though legend has it that they crawl out from under rocks, are actually fairly clean, as creatures go. So, you see, you can't really tie poor Salamandorff to this reptilian comparison on the grounds of hygiene."

"But there's something sinister and slimy about him," she persisted desperately. "He makes my skin crawl. You'll see. In time you'll see what I'm talking about!"

"It's the name, my child," Dinir said soothingly. "You have been bewitched by a name and an idea."

Perhaps Laura's "idea" sprang in part from Salamandorff's way of entering a room in stages, first jutting nose, then thrusting cliff of chin, then curved and craggy shoulders. And always those glistening bead eyes, staring out as if from some dark cave. His method of making progress over any distance was to inch and sidle, silently, so that he often came upon people unaware, almost as if he had appeared spontaneously on the spot. Laura, leaning intently over her slides, sometimes looked up to find him breathing heavily behind her and making an odd licking sound with his tongue.

"I come to peruse the work of our lady scientist," he'd hiss in his strange, sibilant accent, his face so close to hers that she could feel the heat of his breath. "I myself am engaged in a most delectable experiment. Come to my room sometime and I will elaborate." When he spoke, a pale teardrop of saliva would invariably appear at the corner of his absurdly grinning mouth.

"Go away!" Laura screamed at him one day. "Go away and leave me alone! I detest you!"

"Yes, yes, I go, fair lady, I fly," he hissed, backing away with strange, hunching motions.

But her efforts to repulse him only seemed to make him more determinedly attracted to her. She never knew when she would turn to find his sly, grinning face behind her, his tongue softly clicking in appreciation. He was around every corner and in back of every door, perversely beckoning with his skeleton's fingers, until the threat of his presence became like a crushing weight. Often, as she sat at her work, she would feel a familiar chill run up her spine and prickle the hairs on her neck, and she would know that he was there again.

"You've got *to do* something," she beseeched Dinir in a wailing voice. "Yesterday I caught him standing behind me, stroking my hair with those horrible clammy hands of his. And when I scream at him to go away, he makes an awful gurgling sound in his throat and slithers out like a lizard. He's stalking me, I tell you, for what end I can't bear to think!"

"My dear girl, the man comes to us with the most exemplary credentials," Dinir assured her, pretending not to be alarmed by her hysteria, "and I have no doubt that his work here will prove to be imminently worthwhile." He poured a drop of fine white powder onto a slide and gently tapped at the glass with his forefinger. A long moment passed, filled with the sound of Laura's panting inhalations, before he looked up with a soft, paternal smile and said, "You share the fate of *all* beautiful women, you know, in that you provide an irresistible attraction for the more-homely specimens of the race. The desire for the utterly unattainable. Perverse, you might say, but there it is."

As this seemed to be his final word on the subject, she never spoke of it again, though her obsession with Salamandorff grew in direct proportion to his own obsession with her, until they were trapped in a dreadful stalemate. Eventually even Dinir, patiently seeking oblivion through his work, could not help noticing the awful change in her. Her face was pale and haggard, as if

165

from sleeplessness, and her eyes had the vacant, staring look of the hunted. Indeed, she was forever glancing over her shoulder as she stumbled through the large, quiet rooms like someone drunk or in a trance. Dinir thought that he really must do something about it, tomorrow, or the next day, or whenever there was time. He would speak to Salamandorff, tactfully pointing out that his pursuit of Laura was a hopeless one and must, for the sakes of all concerned, be ceased.

So ludicrous, after all, that these emotional exercises should be carried out in a scientific laboratory!

After a while, through some convulsive rebellion against fear, Laura began to actively seek out her pursuer; the suspense of waiting for him to find her was so intolerable that she often felt that she must find him first and get it over with. The result was that she and Salamandorff were occasionally to be seen peering at each other around corners or through the small, glass panes of the laboratory doors. And always, when this happened, he would smile his sinister, oily smile at her and send her fleeing.

One midnight, she crept to his laboratory at the end of a long, dark hallway, drawn there by a glimmer of light and a consuming curiosity about her tormentor. She leaned against the cool, white door, listening to a peculiar scratching sound within and to Salamandorff's sibilant whispering. "Shoo,

166

shoo, my sweets," she heard him whistling. "Into the box, until tomorrow."

Just as she was getting up the courage to look through the glass, the door was flung open and he grasped her roughly by the arm. "Come in, my love. I've been waiting for you," he whispered. He was even more disheveled than usual. His long white laboratory coat was hideously stained, and his hair was flying wildly about his coarse, manic face. Rivers of sweat ran in the creases of his brow, and his fingers, pressing into the softness of her inner arm, felt hot and gritty.

She tried to draw away, but the bony fingers tightened like a vise around her wrist and she was pulled inside.

Dinir found her the next morning, a crunch of clothing on the floor, wildly batting at her face and breasts. "Lizard! Lizard!" she was screaming, and, indeed, a small white lizard crawled out from under her skirt and madly scratched its way across the polished floor. Dinir, however, didn't think that was the one her screams referred to.

Salamandorff was gone, of course, vanished into a malignant obscurity. And because Laura never spoke again, no one ever knew what really happened, though Dinir thought he had a pretty good idea, at least enough to make a scientific guess. He felt the full force of guilt and remorse upon him as he watched her being gently led away, howling one last time, "Lizard!"

He abandoned his work then and

disappeared, fleeing from his crime of neglect. When he emerged a few years later, he had been transformed by his exile into a gaunt and wild-eyed old man, only half scientist now and more than half magician. He began to lurk in the shadows of the scientific world, turning up occasionally at symposiums where the bright young scientists who had never heard of him regarded him as an atavistic relic of the dark ages of alchemy and necromancy. He once invaded a gathering of rocket scientists, declaring that he had designed a pyramid-shaped rocket which could be propelled in an infinite outward journey, fueled only by a tiny box of solar energy near its apex; the obscure reasoning being that the geometric perfection of the pyramid, together with the solar energy, provided an irresistible attraction to the outer planets. The distinguished scientists listened politely for a quarter of an hour and then, having abruptly adjourned the meeting, rose and fled the room as though there were a time bomb ticking in it, leaving Dinir standing forlornly in his frayed gray coat, a chaos of charts and graphs spread out upon the table before him.

Through all these years he searched for Laura, driven by an agony of conscience and some nebulous intent. She had been shifted about among a variety of institutions, some barbaric and some humane, like a crumpled package with the wrong address. A bit of human flotsam which no one knew quite how to dispose of.

Dinir found her at last, about ten years after that bizarre morning in the laboratory, residing for the moment in a relatively civilized sanitarium near the ocean. When he was shown into her room, a small, pale-green cubicle, she was walking blankly in a circle, around and around, her head bent low and her arms hanging limply at her sides. She was a silent, stalking ghost of a woman now, with milky-white, staring eyes and dumb, quivering lips. All the grace was gone from her once exquisite form as she shambled, dragging one foot heavily behind the other, in the ugly, sterile room with cross-barred window. One could almost hear the chains clanking as she walked.

"She's been doing that for weeks," remarked a white-coated attendant, in the manner of discussing, with some annoyance, a strain of bad weather. "The other patients complain at night about her clomp, clomp, clomping around in here. We even handcuffed her to the bed one night, but she just sat up on the edge and clomped her feet anyway, like she was up and walking in her circle as usual. And the sedatives don't really help much either. She fights them like a demon. She's a strong old dame."

"No, she isn't," said Dinir quietly. "Neither strong nor old nor a 'dame'."

He watched her, fascinated, as she traveled in her endless revolutions, marking out a universe of planets on the floor. If she saw or recognized him, she gave no indication; she may as well have been a carrot for all the intelligence revealed in her mushy, vegetable face.

"Send for the doctors," commanded Dinir imperiously, "the chief of staff, the head shrinker of heads, the top administrator, the accountant – *anyone* in a position of authority! And get him here at once," he said, suddenly turning his black, magician's eyes upon the helpless lackey, who went scurrying off without another word, probably scouting for empty rooms along the way in which to incarcerate the tall, gray-coated visitor.

It was some twenty minutes – Dinir breathing fire from his nostrils during this impertinent and injudicious wait – before a short, stout, bespectacled, child-man came slouching in, his fat, freckled hands shoved defensively into the pockets of his hip-length smock.

"Doctor Belvedere, staff psychiatrist," he mumbled, in that bored and offhand way which doctors are required to master before leaving medical school. "What can I do for you?" he sighed with infinite weariness.

"Not what you can do for *me*," said Dinir in a startling hiss, as he spun in a whirlwind arc which sent his coattails flying, "but what you can do for *her*. She is walking in a circle. You see?"

"Of course, I see. We've all seen. She's been doing it ever since she came. She's in a traumatic withdrawal and she likes to walk in circles. So, what?"

"She is attempting to discover and create her own *mandala*," breathed Dinir, enunciating the syllables as if speaking to a foreigner or a small child. "Her *mandala*, which is the circle of her essence and existence."

"Don't give me any of that Jungian nonsense," snorted Belvedere. "This is a mental institution, not some kind of cultish commune. We deal with crazy people here."

Dinir took a step or two, hunched and menacing, toward the doctor, whose face contorted into a bulbous question mark.

"She is seeking, within the mysterious depths of this circle, to find and free her demons, so that her conscious mind may live again, unchained and un-imprisoned by certain secrets which lay hidden in the lonely abyss of the *sub*conscious. You understand? Of course, you do, being a physician of the psyche. And that is why she walks in a circle, drawing, planning, perfecting her mandala.

"Bring in a lizard!"

"What?" screeched Belvedere, the portly psychiatrist. "Are you out of your mind – excuse the expression, it's an occupational hazard - but a *lizard*? Whatever for?"

Dinir ignored the outburst and bent to place his sprawling hand upon the young doctor's shoulder, like a wise, old mentor preparing to speak to his callow protege.

"There is a *lizard* in her past," he said, speaking into the doctor's face in a hushed and reverent tone. "And the lizard holds the key, the *only* key, which can unlock the secrets of the past and set her free.

"Get it at once," he said, "just a small one - probably you've got dozens crawling about unseen in the garden - and bring it here to me immediately. I'll wait."

"Well, I don't know, I really don't," stammered the beleaguered Belvedere. "I'd have to check with my colleagues first, of course." He began backing out of the room, his saucer eyes devouring the splendid spectacle of the ghostly, circling woman and the gray-clad, black-eyed wizard.

"Then do so at once, dear doctor," prodded Dinir with feigned patience, "and let us get on with healing this unfortunate woman. That is, after all, why you are employed here, is it not?"

Belvedere retreated, nodding, having pulled his hands from the protective pockets in order to hold them clasped together, in an attitude of prayer.

Dinir paced up and down the floor beside Laura, studying her, bending now and then to try to get a glimpse into her slack and unresponsive face. Their two figures, moving slowly and deliberately about the small room, seemed to be doing a kind of ritual, cadence dance - she, walking in the ceaseless, trance-like circle, while he marked a short, straight path beside her.

"My dear girl, do not fear. I have come to help you," he whispered in a soothing, sing-song voice. "We will find your demon and release it. And it will never bother you anymore."

He may as well have talked to the wall or the ragged curtains, for her pale blue, watery eyes never looked at him, never showed the slightest flicker of light or expression. There seemed to be no mind behind them anymore.

"You must destroy the lizard," he urged. "You must murder it as it has tried to murder you, your soul."

Half an hour passed in this way, Dinir stoutly keeping his vigil beside her, though he had grown very weary and had begun to drag somewhat, unconsciously falling into her same shambling gait. At one point, a thin, ugly woman in an apron entered, slammed a tray upon the table and exited without a word. The sight of the remarkable duo was nothing new to her; she had lost all capacity for curiosity. The tray contained a plate of food, small portions of some lumpy, indistinguishable fare. Dinir lifted the white ceramic plate and held it up to Laura, gently coaxing her to try a bite or two. But she continued, in her rhythmic, circling course, to brush past him, completely inattentive to his pleading efforts, and when he came too close, the plate was knocked from his hands and fell to the floor in a messy pile. He gathered it up as best he could, replaced the tray upon the table and sank onto the bed with a sigh of exhaustion and despair.

Still more minutes went by, almost an hour now, Dinir merely staring blankly at Laura from his post on the bed, confounded for once and even a bit alarmed. Suddenly a

173

panting figure appeared in the doorway, Dr. Belvedere, breathing heavily and clutching a tiny cardboard box to his chest. "I've got it," he whispered conspiratorially, his face a collage of helplessness and fright.

"The lizard?"

"Yes. It took me forever to find one, and then the blasted thing kept slipping away. They're disgusting, slippery creatures. Dear God, I hope I wasn't seen. They'll be putting me in one of the rooms if I was."

"And did you consult with your colleagues?"

"No, I thought it best not to, after all. This is most unorthodox, you understand?"

"Orthodoxy is never a cure, merely a hiding place, said Dinir fiercely.

"Oh, I don't know *why* I'm doing this," sighed the poor doctor helplessly, as Dinir came forward to relieve him of his loathsome treasure.

Dinir reached into the box and pulled out a small, greenish-brown lizard, holding it by the tail as it squirmed and leapt upward, arching against gravity in its effort to get free. A trail of saliva-like substance dripped from its foaming mouth.

"*Precisely,*" he said, with satisfaction.

While the doctor looked on in anguish, Dinir crept surreptitiously into the center of Laura's circle, crouched and dropped the lizard, then stepped quickly backward out of her line of travel. The creature scratched at the floor and crawled around in a confused circumference, imitating her actions. It was clearly dazed and kept making futile little leaps in the air, only to land with a thud upon the floor once more.

For the first time since Dinir had entered the room, Laura stopped, stood breathlessly still and twisted her head to look at the lizard at her feet. It was impossible to tell if she was really seeing it, for her face remained the same blank page. Though she *must* have seen it, must have taken note of it in some deep recess of her addled brain, or why else would she have halted her insistent, aimless wandering?

Suddenly she took a step backward and stomped the thing with her foot, crushing its back. Then she stepped away and stood staring down at it, a faint glimmer of sinister expression in her eyes at last.

"You see?" shouted Dinir triumphantly. "It is done! She is cured!"

"Oh, my god," cried Belvedere, unable to remove his gaze from the lurid heap on the floor. "You're as crazy as she is!

"Get out of here!" he screamed. "Get out! Get out! Get out!"

Dinir dropped a card on the table and flew from the room, smiling. He never saw Laura again, for he was convinced, in his own muddled mind, that he had cured her forever of her dreadful and tormenting illness.

He had not, of course, and she remained an inmate of the shabby, claustrophobic

175

room, still traveling in circles as she stared out through leaden eyes. The only residual effect of his remarkable "cure" seemed to be that she would now sometimes stop in mid-circle, step suddenly forward and slap the floor with her foot, uttering a hoarse, croaking laugh as she did. Poor Belvedere, whenever he witnessed this, would be heard to emit a long, low moan. He was in sad decline.

Dinir, on the other hand – having cast off the oppressive weight of his guilt – began to thrive once more. He resumed his work in a modest way and, through a sort of gradual rehabilitation, eventually redeemed himself among his peers. Now and then he would muse over the dark years of exile and aberration, not so much distressed by the recollection as simply perplexed. But soon even that began to recede, grew dimmer and dimmer and was gone. And with it, all conscious memory of Laura.

Until one late Autumn evening.

Dinir, as always, was crouched before his microscope, delirious with the expectation of an imminent breakthrough in his work, when he heard a soft tapping on the outer door.

"Come in, come in," he barked, without looking up. "Good god, why can't they leave me alone," he muttered, and carefully selected a slide.

There was no sound of opening door or footfall and yet all at once he felt as if a cold, sharp wind had been allowed into the room; he could even hear its whistling

176

breath behind him. Dinir gave one great, convulsive shudder and dropped the slide to the counter with a tinkling crash.

He twirled around to find a vision of grotesque humanity standing in the doorway, a towering ruin of a body in ragged clothes. The features of the stark, ravaged face were almost completely obliterated by a dense growth of matted, yellowish hair. Only the eyes showed clearly, dark bead eyes in which little fires of incredible intensity still danced and leapt. Fires which were apparently unquenchable.

"Salamandorff!" cried Dinir in a raspy voice. And it all came down upon him again, the nightmare and the horror, like an annihilating avalanche. "You devil! You curse of God! You unspeakable monster!" he howled, lurching forward in a blind fury. "You worm of worms, how do you dare to walk among men?" some alien voice within him shouted, as he raised two fists to pound upon the hollow chest before him. For a moment, only the dull, thudding sound of his pounding fists was heard in the room, and then a ghastly and inhuman cry, a sound dredged up from some bottomless pit of despair, tore through the air and echoed back from every corner.

Salamandorff had dropped to his knees and thrown both frail and bony arms about Dinir's legs. "Yes, yes," he hissed, "I am a worm, I am a *monster*. I have no right to live," he wailed, through loud, wrenching sobs. Dinir, looking down in horror, took a step backward, only to drag the pathetic,

177

clutching fingers with him.

"I come seeking absolution for my crime!" cried Salamandorff, his sibilant wailing growing louder and louder. "It has driven me to every corner of the earth and I can find no rest. You must set me *free!*"

Finally, with an effort, Dinir raised one leg and kicked him away. "You will receive no absolution from me," he growled, "you destroyer and defiler." He felt as if he had lapsed into a terrible dream.

It occurred to him fleetingly that he could reach behind him to grasp the vial of acid on the counter and dispense with Salamandorff once and for all. A simple, reasonable act, done in the name of humanity. But when he gazed down on the decrepit form crouched like a beggar at his feet, all his own guilt came flooding back into his brain until he grew faint with it.

"I cannot help you," he said, and turned sharply away, for he could no longer bear to look on Salamandorff. "Any forgiveness for your unspeakable deed must come from Laura, your victim, and I have already undone your ghastly handiwork." When he spoke these words, he was startled by the sudden recollection of the absurd episode in the sanitarium. Had he really done that? And if he had, had he really believed in it? It all seemed so distant and unreal, so utterly unconnected to his present life.

"Then tell me where she is!" Salamandorff cried out wildly, as he scrambled across the floor on all fours. "I will go to her and beg her forgiveness, so that I may live again!" His voice was like a hissing screech now.

Dinir was afraid that he might try to grasp his legs again and so walked hurriedly to the far side of the counter. As he stood there, listening with one ear to Salamandorff's sickening pleas, he ran his fingers lightly over the smooth surfaces of the glass tumblers and the slides, caressed the rough-textured base of his microscope and looked with longing at the furry culture growing in a small pan.

He wanted desperately to be done with Salamandorff and with Laura - with *all* of it. He had paid a terrible price already for their collaboration as victim and tormentor, having reclaimed his own sanity through an excruciating effort.

It *must* not rest on his shoulders any longer.

"I really don't know where she is. I can only tell you where I last saw her," he said, reaching for a scrap of paper on which he scribbled the name of the sanitarium where he and Laura and Dr. Belvedere had played out their comic scene. "But I doubt very much that you'll find her there. It was years ago, and she was then well on her way to being whole again," he said, astonished to hear himself uttering this specious prognosis.

Salamandorff remained where he was on the floor a moment, making a sound like a whimpering dog. Then he rose awkwardly to his feet, knocking over a stool in his upward progress, and leaned across the counter to whisper into the other man's face, "Bless you, bless you, Dinir. I will find her and beg her forgiveness, and we will *both* be whole again."

Dinir drew back just as the clawing, bony fingers reached out to touch him.

It was over for him, again and at last, and with hardly a moment's pause, he passed once more into the serene oblivion of his work. Whenever he did think of it, which was seldom, the cosmic struggle between Salamandorff and Laura seemed like nothing so much as a second-rate Greek tragedy, with all the trappings. Well, he was done playing the role of the bumbling, interceding god in their absurd drama. It had been a fool's part at best.

But the play was not quite over yet, it seemed.

It must have the grisly epilogue which occurred a few weeks after Salamandorff's unpropitious visit, when Dinir answered the telephone to hear a timorous and vaguely reminiscent voice: "Dr. Belvedere, here. I'm only calling because I thought you'd want to know."

Dinir resisted fiercely the sudden downward plunge of all his senses. He didn't want to know - *whatever* it was, he didn't want to know.

"We've had a most unfortunate incident here involving your friend. As you were the only other one who ever came to see her, I really thought you should be informed.

"Had a *helluva* time finding out how to reach you, by the way," added Belvedere, petulantly.

"What has happened?" Dinir asked in a toneless voice, though he really thought he knew.

"Well, it's absolutely incredible," said Belvedere, warming to his narrative, "but some pathetic derelict appeared here the other day and asked to see her. I must say, the poor woman seems to have led a very strange life before she came to us, by the look of her companions. No offense meant, of course," he added halfheartedly.

"Yes, yes, get on with it," barked Dinir.

"Well, the point is, she's killed him."

He let his revelation have the moment's silence it deserved, savoring the sound of Dinir's labored breathing at the other end, before he spoke again. "Naturally, we've had to take rather drastic measures, to insure such a thing won't happen again, to render her harmless, so to speak. It's very odd, because there was no indication before that she was homicidal. But then, one never knows with these poor creatures."

Dinir had a fleeting vision of Laura in her prime; he saw her tremulous, dark beauty and heard her whispering lushly in his ear, "The man reminds me of a *lizard*."

"How did it happen?" he asked, too numb to care.

"Well, that's the really amazing part," said Belvedere with barely concealed glee. "He was a terribly frail old man, on his

181

last legs, I'd say. And she was very strong, as the insane quite often are. And, to put it simply, it seems that she threw him onto the floor and stomped him to death."

12 OCTOBER FIRE

Kathryn was sure she had only glanced away for a moment, tempted by the colorful window display – and in the speck of time, the unthinkable happened!

She had forgotten the hole in the pocket of her worn jacket, only remembering when she heard the car keys plink to the ground before the window of a small boutique. As she plucked the keys from the pavement, she stole a quick glance at the autumn fashions on show amid an artful display of pumpkins, miniature haystacks and brightly-colored autumn leaves, her eyes lingering briefly on a soft suede jacket which would have made an admirable replacement for the threadbare tweed she was wearing. The suede was of a creamy beige color which would complement her pale, flawless skin and deep-set umber eyes, and would provide a perfect contrast for the thick chestnut hair which fell about her shoulders in a soft, unfettered style...

But better not to think of things you couldn't have, she'd thought wistfully, turning away.

Tucking the keys into her purse for safety, she reached out in a gesture as automatic as breathing to take Charlotte's hand once more –

...and found the child was nowhere in sight!

Kathryn sucked in her breath, her eyes darting frantically to left and right in hope of seeing her daughter's tousled blond head nearby. It was so "Charlie" to wander away without warning, her uninhibited spirit as-yet oblivious to the many dangers the world presented to a small, defenseless child.

As a single mother, Kathryn was only too aware of the fine line she must tread between reasonable precaution and over-protectiveness, between allowing Charlotte the freedom to discover the world without fear and suffocating her with warnings.

How could she keep her daughter safe, she'd asked herself a thousand times, without destroying the childlike trust which was at once Charlie's most endearing quality and her mother's constant source of anxious dread?

Now she was gone! Just like that! Kathryn's mind filled with images of milk cartons emblazoned with the poignant smiles of missing children, the distraught faces of sobbing parents on the evening news...

How did they bear it! she had always wondered. How could *anyone* bear to lose a child under any circumstances, but especially in a manner which was never resolved, leaving one to linger indefinitely between hope and despair...? And Kathryn knew that Charlotte's unquenchable zest for life made her especially vulnerable; the child simply didn't know the *meaning* of the word "stranger".

But she had never disappeared before!

Blinking away tears as she fought against a rising hysteria, Kathryn began to walk on wobbly legs along the nearly deserted street, peering desperately into shop windows whose bright inviting displays might have attracted the curious five-year-old. But it was just past six and most of the shops and businesses were closed for the day, their shuttered facades seeming to mock her frantic scrutiny.

Oh, God, please let her be all right! Please let me find her! she prayed against the furious thumping of her heart.

All at once she heard a familiar giggle from across the street. Relief surging through her, Kathryn wheeled around - only to find herself confronted by every parent's worst nightmare!

For here, on the opposite pavement, was Charlie, all right - but she was not alone! A strange man was kneeling before her, one hand on her tiny shoulder as he offered candy with the other.

"Charlie! Don't...!" Kathryn yelled, her legs feeling like jelly as she dodged the slow-moving traffic and reached her daughter in a breathless dash.

"Mommy, Mommy... look what I got!" Charlie exclaimed, her face lit like a Christmas tree as she held forth a brightly-wrapped lollipop for Kathryn's inspection.

Kneeling, Kathryn pulled her daughter into her arms and held her tight against her racing heart. "Oh, Charlie, Charlie... you frightened me so much! I didn't know where

185

you'd gone to. Don't ever do that to mommy again."

"Perhaps if you'd been paying attention to your child, instead of admiring the clothes in that shop window, she wouldn't have wandered off in the first place."

Kathryn looked up in disbelief at the looming figure of the stranger, only to find him staring down at her with a gaze so piercing it almost made her flinch.

How dare he accuse her in this way? *He* was the transgressor here, offering candy to an innocent child.... What kind of monster was he, anyway?

Taking a deep breath to still the desperate pounding of her heart, she rose from the pavement and faced him, keeping one hand protectively on Charlie's furry brown head. "Look, I don't know who you are or what your intention was in offering candy to my daughter," she said, her voice raspy with anger and the aftermath of terror, "but I hardly think that you are in any position to take that indignant tone with me. For all I know, you were trying to lure her away for some unspeakable purpose," she said with deceptive calmness, feeling her cheeks burning with confused emotion.

Towering above her, the man had the wholesome, rugged good looks of one who spends a great deal of time outdoors, an impression not belied by the well-worn jeans, khaki shirt and scuffed but expensive-looking boots he wore. Not exactly her image of the sleazy type who preys on children, she thought hastily, then reminded herself that, of course, there was no particular profile for a child molester.

But there was something about this man made such a judgment seem almost impossible, a kind of stern self-composure – almost a steely reserve - which would have been nothing short of remarkable if he had indeed just been thwarted in the middle of such a vile act.

Charlie tugged fiercely at her hand. "Mommy, the man was nice to me," she said in a bewildered voice. "He gave me a lollipop and said he'd take me across the street to find you."

Kathryn rose slowly from the pavement and looked up into two brilliant blue eyes which seemed to burn through her like laser beams. "Is that correct? *Were* you just trying to help her?"

He ran a hand through thick, sun-bleached hair and sighed, as though from exhaustion. "I happened to notice the two of you standing before the boutique, and when you turned away your little girl darted across the street. She barely avoided being hit by a passing car," he added accusingly. Kathryn's hand shot to her heart at the picture his words painted. If anything happened to Charlie...

"When I saw you running down the street in search of her, I called out to you but apparently you didn't hear me," he went on. "And before I could bring her to you, you came marching over here to accuse me of trying to abduct your child."

"Look... I'm... I'm sorry," Kathryn stammered in embarrassment. "But surely you understand how frightened I was when I saw her talking to a stranger. One hardly knows who to trust anymore."

He gave a snort of derisive laughter. "Did we ever?"

13 SPIDER WEBS

"I see it rising as a monument to mediocrity," the old man said, scratching with his witch's fingers at the air, "a symbol of all the evanescent dreams which blur our vision and all the inarticulate hopes which choke in our throats." He melted deep into the pillow until only his gray face showed, as though his head were floating on a sea of white water. "My wall... my lovely wall," he spoke through a reverent exhalation. "Made not of bottle caps and broken tile and bits of garbage.

"But what better to tell the story, eh?" he asked, and his head turned upon his neck like a rusty screw.

"Don't be crazy, Poppa," pleaded Marcus. "You're an old man, you're sick, you'll die if you don't take care." He looked beyond a pale green curtain at the silhouetted trees outside, away from his father's smile and fluttering fingers.

His father had never seemed so old or ugly, he thought, as he did at that moment, with all the faltering machinery of his human mechanism grinding to a final halt – and *still* that gleam of madness in his eyes! It had pursued Marcus all his life, that embarrassed look - that inexplicable and slightly fiendish glint - through embarrassed boyhood into tremulous maturity,

189

like a searing sun spot on the back of his neck.

"But I'll die *anyway*, whether I take care or not," said the old man, and a spasm of dry, rasping laughter rattled the stillness of the antiseptic room. "There is no higher court to take it to; all my appeals, like all my money, have been spent.

"And for *what*?" he asked, straining upward until the veins in his neck and marbled temples stood out like swollen tributaries, blue and bulging. "For pills and treatments and prescriptions, all the useless artifices of modern *technique*, which strives to keep a man alive beyond the waning of his gifts and powers." He closed his eyes and through the thin, crepey sheaths of lids, Marcus could see his father's eyes roll up and back. "They care very much for us at the end, don't they?" the old man spoke in a whisper of hoarse intensity which frightened his son, had always frightened him. "Oh, yes, indeed, they care very much at the end. To prove something, perhaps?" And another dry gust of rattling laughter parched the room.

"Hush, now, Poppa," said Marcus, begrudging his affection. "Lie back and go to sleep, for God's sake." His hand, as it played along the white sheet, tucking in the crisp, starchy corners, trembled with an organic anger which only his strenuously achieved sense of civilized behavior held in check.

"You will finish my wall for me, won't you, Marcus, my son?" the old man whispered.

He was settling back into the bed a limb at a time, sliding his bare-branch legs beneath the covers like a rustle of dead leaves, easing the skeleton elbows out along the chafing sheet.

Marcus blinked at the tubes and bottles hanging just above his father's head and rang for a nurse.

Of course, his father had *always* been crazy, he thought, with some little sense of comfort, triumph, even. Doctor, lawyer, Indian chief. Writer, painter and Utopian schemer. The old man, in his prime, had tried to be them all, with small success, until he had made himself at last into one thing: a ludicrous collage. A hopeless layering of dreams piled upon one another in a quiltwork pattern so that the man beneath the dreams was lost, to all be himself. And that was the one, great, indigestible question: Why had his father never sensed his failure? And how could he help but see beneath his own facade? The answer, Marcus felt, was locked in that maniacal and flinty cast of eyes.

Crazy!

But even so, what to make of this wall? This obscene eruption on a concrete partition in a ghetto? His father, dying, bereft of wife and manly strength and all his dreams not merely dead but buried beneath the crushing weight of ridicule, had begun a "mural" on the wall behind his one-bedroom apartment in a stucco duplex, in an

191

area long ago surrendered to poverty and despair. With pieces of brown cellophane torn from bread wrappers, bottle caps and bits of broken glass, magazine covers, and scavenged garbage taken on midnight raids from clanging barrels, he was attempting to tell the story of Man's evolution from the darkness of the depths of the sea as he crawled up and outward onto dry land, flinging the loggy moisture from his scales in pursuit of - what? Truth? Beauty? Peace of Mind?

As if a little imagination and epoxy glue could tell the story, could make it comprehensible!

But then, his father had never been known for practicality. Far from it. "If dreams were money, I'd be rich," he liked to say, sometimes laughing and sometimes with a lemon drop of sorrow in his voice. He must have set some kind of record, Marcus thought, for going bankrupt in hare-brained business schemes. There was the "Poor Man's Art Gallery", housed in a crumbling barn in the middle of nowhere, whose patrons, of course, were too poor to buy the art even if it had been worth buying. And the private school for gifted children, closed by police when the "gifted" children were discovered selling the school's supplies, even the furniture from the dormitory, to the good citizens of a nearby town. And most notable of all, the frog farm. "Just think of something people want and give it to them," he'd say simply, and at some point, he concluded that people wanted frog's legs.

Which might have been the case, but they were never to know, for a drenching Spring rain poured down into the homemade "pond" he had dug too deeply in a pasture from behind the house, and all the frogs drowned in a sea of muddy water.

A week after Marcus's mother died – from anger and exhaustion, he was sure - he and his father set off across the country, living in little spurts in different places, like traveling actors, discarding towns and occupations as easily as costumes. And then one summer, when he was twelve, they settled into a comfortably creaky old house on ten acres of neglected farmland in central Texas. "A man must dig with his hands into the earth, to find his own roots," his father said majestically, playing farmer for the moment. They grew some corn and okra and tomatoes and kept a company of squabbling chickens in the backyard. In the fall they bought a speckled cow, and Marcus knew the dubious thrill of pulling warm milk from her belly with his own hands. He walked to school along a dirt road, dressed in jeans and flannel shirts, and stopped at Smith's Grocery in the afternoons for a cold drink and some talk with the other boys, and felt at home, at last. He would have been content to stay in that place, lingering in rust-brown fields to watch the day-long spectacle of ants parading through the grass, or lying beneath an arching willow in the front yard to observe the slow dissolution of clouds in clear skies. He took deep breaths in that place and he was never late for anything; for Time was a glistening jewel-drop suspended in the air.

It burst one afternoon when his father snatched him up and away with a peremptory speech about "new worlds to conquer," and they had moved on again.

That was when he knew his father for a fool.

He took the long way home from the hospital, skirting the narrow, trashy streets which might have brought him close to his father's latest crude, humiliating venture. He had not seen the wall yet, had only heard the old man's rambling and monomaniacal descriptions of it. Six inches tall! Two feet high! Four feet, and man not only upright now but stretching beyond the towering buildings of his own design - which were made of cardboard and cloth and bits of gluey thread - and reaching upward to the stars!

Imagine! This *thing*, creeping up one side of a wall in a blackened alley in a no-man's land of furious contempt! Either a fungus or a miracle, depending upon one's point of view.

Marcus slammed shut the door to his apartment with a thunderous crunch and headed for the bathroom, leaving a trail of flung clothing in the intervening rooms. He would wash away his father's lush excesses and his own humiliation - even *death* - in a tub of hot, cleansing water. He twisted the silver knobs at the head of the tub and watched as the violent streams of purging water poured into the porcelain basin, rushing like boiling waves to the farther end and sending up a fine mist of comforting, obliterating warmth. But just as he was about to place one trepid toe into the water, he noticed, from the outer limits of peripheral vision, a small black speck scrambling up and away from the steamy deluge, slipping and sliding on the glassy smoothness of the tub in a feverish orgasm of survival instinct.

It was a spider, a coarse, black, hairy thing, whose nettled, scrabbling legs showed him more of desperation in that moment than he had learned in a lifetime.

For some reason he didn't understand - would *never* understand - he lunged forward and, with a frantic scuffling at the knobs, cut off the water. Then he reached behind him to snatch a damp and crinkled copy of the *Wall Street Journal* from the toilet cover and retrieved the creature, scooping it up and away from its watery fate and placing it on the great expanse of snowy plain which was the corner of the tub. It wandered blindly, dazed, into the tiled wall, backed off and settled into a crumpled heap on the slippery porcelain shelf, drawing its feathery legs beneath it.

And just above, glistening like penciled outlines in the harsh glare of light, a viscid, silvery web of crossed threads was growing on the wall, halfway up the length

195

of humid tile. A thing of such intense fragility and softness, Marcus thought, that one might pull it down with one finger and feel nothing.

The spider arched its furry back and moved in slow motion to the web, raising a spindly leg as if to scale the wall once more; but it could get no hold and slid down into a small black pool on the white tub each time it tried.

Marcus watched a moment, wondering if it were passionate desire or dumb instinct which drove the creature on, repeatedly, to sure defeat. Then he eased the spider onto the newspaper and lifted it up again, placing it on the wall where it had left off working on its web. The spider resumed its work at once, drawing out the pencil lines of thread in slow, deliberate movements dredged up from its very body.

It occurred to Marcus that the web should have reached the ceiling by tomorrow night, and he slipped cautiously into a shallow depth of water in the tank.

"You see, son," the old man was saying in a crone's voice, struggling to rise upon one frail elbow, "I see it as a panoramic view of man's relentless journey to the stars, which is a euphemism for the dreams we nurture in silence, because we're afraid to tell anyone."

His laughter was a little thinner now

196

than Marcus remembered it from childhood, with all the sharp, cutting edges rounded off by age and illness and defeat.

"Dr. Kaiser says you won't take your medicine or eat your food," Marcus said in a monotone, trying to give an appearance of not caring.

"Food, food, food," said the old man disparagingly, rolling his sweaty head from side to side on the moist pillow. "I've eaten food all my life. So what else is new? I'm trying to tell you something, goddammit!

"Will you listen for one minute in forty years?" he said, flinging his butterfly fingers into the air.

Marcus looked through the open window at a soft wash of amber twilight, wishing he were outside, wishing he were anywhere but here. An old evocation.

"What is it, Poppa?" he asked, and his hands trembled in his lap. "What do you want to tell me?"

"That you must finish my wall, goddammit," urged the old man. "It can be a work of Art, a thing of truth and beauty, only I haven't time... I haven't time to do it all myself." He choked on the words, and Marcus pushed him back against the pillow, smoothing his forehead and damp cheeks with his own warm fingers.

"There's a little spot in the left-hand corner, you know," the old man said softly, after a moment, "where I show Da Vinci creating the airplane. Put the final touches to that, will you? A little green and gold? Those empty boxes of ladies' hair coloring

197

are good for that." Then he grew pale again and sank into the pillow, his cheeks descending like chalk caverns into the blue-ridged labyrinths of his face. He looked up through rheumy, water-color eyes. "You will do that for me, won't you, son?"

"Sure, Poppa, sure," said Marcus, with a little belch of turmoil in his stomach. "Now rest." And he watched his father's eyes close, like shades drawn shut in a museum.

Driving home in the silky night of early evening, Marcus felt as if someone had pulled a plug in his mind, allowing all his strength and will to drain out, drop by drop. The old man had done it to him again!

He had spent the better part of his life escaping from his father, fleeing from all he was and all he represented - the mindless idealism and bravura gestures, the self-indulgent posturing of the Artist in Search of Himself. And in defense against such things, he had cultivated, in his own life, preciseness, substance, feasibility, substituting tangible, short-term goals for any far-reaching objective which his soul might have embraced, but which his pragmatist's mind rejected. Once, in adolescence, he had felt the first warm stirrings of artistic desire and had sat in the velvet darkness of his room, night after night, pouring out his adolescent fears and loneliness into a winding stream of words. And - oh, Lord! - the result was *poetry*. When he realized what he had done, he attributed the aberration to a genetic flaw, passed on from his father, and wrenched it from his heart as if it were a demon. And he had never wavered anymore.

Why, then, must he be brought back after all these years, for a final confrontation with the enemy?

His father hadn't long to live, he was sure. A few weeks, perhaps, or maybe only days. So, was the old man lying in his morbid bed regretting all the injuries he had inflicted on his son, the various thrusts and jabs at soul and dignity? Did he cringe to recall the time he came to Parent's Night at school dressed as a Union soldier, complete with rusty sword and scabbard, to advertise the gaudy Civil War romance he had written and somehow finagled into print? Marcus thought not and tried to hate him, but all that he could conjure up was the sad, gray face and watery eyes and hoarse, bemoaning voice. The cruel thing about the very old, he thought, was that age and imminent death deprived them of their wickedness: They *had* to be forgiven for all the evil deeds committed in their prime, for who could bring himself to punish a shriveled and gray-visage remnant of humanity for *ex post fact* crimes?

He was just turning the key in the front door when he thought of the web, and a slight tingle of anticipation caused him to fling his coat across the couch and head directly for the bathroom. He tried to walk slowly, with a burgeoning sense of foolishness, but somehow the promise of the silvery web's having climbed to the topmost tile in the corner of the bathroom pushed him on, against the grain of his precious self-restraint.

The spider had fallen into the tub once more, however, and was struggling out of its own net of threads, having pulled down most of the web upon itself. Marcus could imagine how the creature must have grasped at the web with its spindly legs in a desperate effort not to fall, only to take its creation plunging with it to the bottom of the tub. A few strands of slender, opaque threads were blowing in the air near the top of the wall, an indication that the web had nearly reached the ceiling.

Marcus felt an irrational surge of anger and contempt for the spider; he had given it a second chance last night, had saved it from extinction at the last moment, only to have it fail again, probably through its own ineptitude and overreaching. Better to be done with the thing once and for all, he thought, and placed his hands on the silver knobs. It would only take a moment to wash the spider down the drain and into oblivion; then he would wipe the remnant threads from the wall, and all traces of the spider would have been erased.

But somehow, he couldn't twist the knobs, at least not yet. For it occurred to him that within this particle of Time and Space, he had the choices of a god; he was all-powerful. He sat on the edge of the tub a moment, flushed with his own omnipotence, then reached and scooped the spider up and gave it back to the wall.

Don't fail again, he warned the creature, in his mind.

But it did, on three more occasions, with the web in various stages of progression up the wall, and three more times Marcus spared it. He would return from the hospital in the evening, his ears and mind still ringing with the old man's death-bed ravings, to find the now familiar scene: the spider in relentless struggle to ascend the glassy smoothness of the tub, sometimes encumbered in its own sticky excretion, and the web now halfway up, now nearly to the ceiling, or pulled down again in a jagged streak. And Marcus felt the frustration as his very own, for he desired the web as fiercely as the spider did. He was no longer a god.

"I know you think I let you down an awful lot," the old man said. His voice was a painful whisper, mined from some bottomless pit in his soul, and little bursts of flame leapt from the corners of his milky eyes. "But it was only because I had a dream, many dreams, and their fulfillment required all my best efforts and attention - I could never stop trying. You do understand, don't you?"

"Of course," said Marcus, lying.

Earlier, when he had listened to the old man ranting about the legendary wall, urging him to complete it, he had noticed with wonderment that the maniacal gleam was still present in his father's eyes, if just barely. That light of madness which could only be extinguished with his father's last breath, he supposed. Amazing!

"Yes, dreams are everything," the old man said, with a tepid flutter of his bony fingers.

"No, they aren't," said Marcus in a murmurous undertone.

"What?"

"I said dreams *are* *not* everything, accomplishment is something. And honest-to-god *accomplishment* now and then." He was startled by the sudden volume of his voice, and its raw edge.

"Sure, sure, accomplishment," said the old man through a harsh laugh. "And what do *you* accomplish, sitting in your office with your stocks and bonds, playing games with other people's money? The world is better off, I suppose, because you make money multiply and rich people richer, eh?"

"At least I have something of value to show for what I do," said Marcus with a panicky feeling that he was careening down a mountain with no brakes.

"Oh, I see," said his father. "So, you think that your paper money has more value than my dreams?"

"Of course, it does!" shouted Marcus. He could hardly get his breath. "For all your half-assed dreams have come to nothing in the end, haven't they? Just like this crazy wall, this... this vertical garbage heap you keep telling me about!"

Why couldn't he stop? Why, oh, why couldn't he stop? He was plunging from the airy heights of kindness and love and custom and taking the old man with him.

"*I* haven't wasted my life in futile efforts, Poppa," he continued, unable to staunch the bloody flow of words, "writing books that no one could bear to read or promoting useless utopian schemes. *I* haven't tried to make clay pots out of clouds."

He sank into his chair and closed his eyes, breathing in short, rapid gulps of air to calm himself. When he looked up, his father was staring at him as if he were a curious phenomenon which had appeared spontaneously in the room.

"Poppa, I...."

"It's all right," said the old man in a husky voice, with a last, pathetic wave of hand. "I understand. You have always hated me."

He found the spider in its usual disarray that night, clamoring up the snow cliff against all sense, insanely. But the web was still intact and nearly reached the ceiling. Marcus went through the motions of their own strange ritual, replacing the spider on the wall, then sat on the rim of the tub and wept.

He arrived at the hospital the next evening just in time to see an army of interns and nurses rushing to his father's room, driving a battery of complex machinery before them. The empty clatter in the corridor was terrifying, and so was the breathless silence which ensued. He stood outside the door and sensed a frantic swishing of hands and a taut murmur of voices within – an eternity of leaden waiting. When it was over, and he was allowed a final visit, he pulled back the sheet from his father's face and raised the crepey lids - he *had* to know - and, yes, the gleam was gone, the eyes were dull and dead.

The last rays of sun were drowning in the western ocean as he parked his car along a grimy side street and went to see his father's wall. It was grotesque and beautiful! A mat of colors and reliefs, made into an exotic facade.

There were rough, twiggy trees and coursing rivers and stark, gray towers pointing toward the sky. There were paper boats and cardboard houses and matchstick men and woman busily evolving, steadfastly climbing upward to what seemed, along the top, to be a panoply of small, aluminum stars against a backdrop of illimitable, airy space. A tiny universe! There were roads made of rope, all leading outward and away, and a glistening rocket ship cut from a tin can and, along the bottom, a midnight ocean of dark blue corduroy, with cresting waves of cotton. And in the upper left-hand corner, bent before a crayon drawing of an "aeroplane," there was a crudely constructed figure in a flowing robe of green and gold. Da Vinci!

Marcus stood back and stared and shook his head. An incoherent jumble of discarded objects pasted on a concrete wall - his father's legacy. An object lesson in sublime futility. But then a street lamp glimmered on and cast the wall in shadow, and the small, aluminum stars, actually seemed to be twinkling in the gauzy night.

"Ain't that somethin'?"

Marcus wheeled around to find a small, dark, dirty creature standing just behind him, a boy of ten or twelve.

"My old man says they must have sent the old guy who did that to the nut house, 'cause he ain't been around in a while."

"No," said Marcus. "He's dead."

"Oh." The boy gazed at the wall in fascination for a moment, squinting to see in the dusky light. "Well, I guess it don't make no difference then," he said at last, "'cause my old man says, they would have made him tear that junk pile down, pretty soon. What do you think?"

"I think," said Marcus, whispering, "that it is a work of art."

He could never remember having driven home that night, the rambling circle down the beach and back into town, to watch the intermingling glow of stars and artificial lights; or the wet slip of moon above the roof at midnight as he thrust the key inside the lock. He could only recall the furious intent with which he marched into the bathroom and removed his shoe, and the one, thudding blow with which he crushed the spider, an inch from the ceiling.

14 <u>OWED TO WILLY YEATS</u>

Did the Irish drive you crazy?
Were they obstinate and lazy?
Was their treatment of you shabby?
Did they desecrate your Abbey
With their vile denunciations
And their Synge-ing condemnations?

We must give you this, poor Willy:
'Tis no wonder you grew silly,
Taking on a mystic's air,
Smelling roses that weren't there,
While you charged your poet's power
In the aerie of your tower.

After all was said and done –
All the races you had run,
All the prizes you had won –
All you wanted was Maud Gonne,
And when you found you hadn't caught her,
Thought you'd settle for her daughter.

Did it suit your sense of symmetry
To woo two branches of a family tree?
T'was all in vain, at any rate:
You wound up wed to Georgie Yeats,
She to whom the spirits spoke
(though some have called it all a joke).

Obsession might have been your curse
If you hadn't turned it into verse.

207

(Did you fantasize an orgy
With Iseult, her Mom and Georgie?
But we'd better not pursue it –
Let's just hope that *you* eschewed it.)

Now your bones are laid to rest –
Earth's, and Auden's, honored guest –
Until, at last, by your own ken,
The spiral spins you back again.
For what it's worth, you passed the test:
You simply were – and are – the best!

15 <u>PERSPECTIVE</u>

He had tumbled from a leaf made slippery by the rain. Riding on a raindrop, he plummeted into a void which seemed to have no end. He lay now on his back, his legs thrusting skyward, flailing against emptiness and space. He had never seen the sky before; his universe consisted of the clumps of earth and blades of grass through which he crawled in search of food. In his amazement, he forgot to struggle but lay motionless a moment, staring into the vastness over him. He had never imagined so much color in the world, so much shape and space and depth; there were dimensions he had never dreamed of. To see it now filled him with both fear and exultation, and he felt that all the moments of his existence had led him to this glimpse of sky.

Suddenly a shadow appeared, a blot of darkness descending inexorably upon him from above, obliterating the undersides of leaves and wisps of cloud and sunlight. In his mind he cried out, pleading for time in which to glimpse the wonder of it all. But it was futile. He heard the crunch of footsteps on the ground - the sound of the world exploding, surely! - and felt himself pressed back into the dirt, enveloped and diffused into the earth from which he'd come....

But he had no regrets... for he had seen the sky.

16 THE BLEEDING ROOM

At noon each day, Bolero Street became a carnival.

First the artists came, flamboyantly attired, to lounge in the flimsy metal chairs of the pavement cafés and sip cheap beer or wine as they discoursed upon the mysteries of existence. Some even brought the fruits of their labors - oil paintings and colorful batiks and handwoven baskets – to display upon the sidewalk for an hour, hoping for a fortuitous sale to pay for lunch. Soon after, roused by the sounds of life below, the bedraggled employees of the offices above the shops poured out into the street, jostling for counter seats at Manito's or Pancho's Villa, if they could afford it, or a vendor's tamales, if they could not.

For an hour or more, the air was made electric with the sounds of exuberant conversations, shouted greetings and the pounding of countless feet upon the sun-scorched pavement, until the artists dispersed reluctantly to their makeshift studios and the workers climbed the stairs once more to their cramped and musty-smelling rooms.

"I beg your pardon," said an unmistakably male voice, though so quietly that she could barely distinguish the words.

211

Clare Lambert had been on her way to the corner market, her head thrust low as she searched for loose change in the bottom of her purse, when she walked into something solid which smelled faintly of tree bark. She was steadied by strong hands grasping her arms, and she looked up into the deepest, darkest eyes she had ever seen.

"I'm afraid I wasn't looking where I was going," he said in that same strange voice, which was barely more than a whisper. He was fortyish, of medium height and build, with swarthy skin and a luxuriance of wavy black hair that Robert, her ex-husband, would have killed for, she thought spitefully. Beneath a thick and drooping black mustache, a smile played briefly on his lips before a cloud descended once more over his curiously somber face.

Clare gasped, not because she was startled, but as she had once gasped in a movie theater, when a dark-haired actor of her fancy took the nubile heroine in his arms and kissed her, setting off an alarming tingling in the pit of Clare's stomach.

But that was twenty years ago, for God's sake, and such inexplicable sensations were inappropriate to a woman of her age. Or so she dutifully told herself, feeling her cheeks grow hot with embarrassment and some other, more disturbing physical reaction.

She stepped back and began making unnecessary brushing motions at her skirt, as though their encounter had soiled her somehow. "It's all right. I wasn't looking

212

where I was going, either," she mumbled, forcing herself to look up at him again and smile. He had the saddest eyes she'd ever seen, and for a giddy moment she was sure that he was seeing through her facade of self-sufficiency to the uncertainty and loneliness beneath.

Then, with a curt nod of his head, he stepped aside and proceeded down the sidewalk in long, slouching strides, a kind of middle-aged "home-boy" walk, thought Clare. She allowed herself one final glance at him and sighed.

Ah, well, back to rummaging for coins.

In the market, which was called a bodega in this neighborhood, she carefully selected a day's worth of supplies – the smallest chunk of Jack cheese available, a load of dark bread, a one-serving can of "chunky" soup and a pack of generic cigarettes – counting out her change upon the dingy counter. When her monthly stipend from the bank arrived, she would gorge on chicken enchiladas and chimichangas at Manito's Cafe around the corner, but for now... well, perhaps a little enforced dieting wouldn't hurt, she thought, pressing one hand against the soft protrusion of her belly.

She loved coming to the bodega, where the air was rich with exotic aromas and the walls reverberated with the chatter of myriad voices, all speaking at once, it seemed, in Spanish and barrio slang. As she waited for her purchases to be bagged by the plump, loquacious woman behind the counter, Clare closed her eyes and listened intently

213

to the language of her new neighborhood, delighted to comprehend a word here and there but mostly with a disparaging sense that she would always be an alien to all by her own small area of the neighborhood known as Parnassus Heights.

When she stepped once more into Bolero Street, she cast a quick glance in the direction of the distant hills, hoping, perhaps, to see, among the bustling throngs, the man with the black hair. But he had vanished, of course, and she wondered if she had only imagined him, had fantasized him into existence for a fleeting moment.

17 <u>THE PEPPER TRICK</u>

I was only seven when my sisters and I first played the pepper trick, but I still recall it as though it were yesterday. It was in a Springtime filled with fireflies and blind man's bluff and picnics on the lawn, a time of innocence that was over all too soon.

I see my father in memory, distilled by the passage of many years, as a tall handsome man with an unruly mop of dark brown hair and sparkling green eyes which seemed always to be smiling. His face was never in repose, in fact; its features were continuously animated by an unquenchable zest for life. He was the happiest person I ever knew, in the despite of having to bring up three little girls all on his own.

Papa was a newspaper reporter. Every evening when he came home from work, he'd gather us around his easy chair and tell us what exciting things had happened that day. About the fire at McGinty's Five and Dime, for instance, when all the plastic fruit got melted. Or about the time when Mr. Jessup's car got stuck on the railroad tracks, just before the 5:14 Express was due. He even told us about the holdup at Bentley's Grocery Store, when two robbers with masks demanded all the cash and a carton of Hershey bars. Papa had quite a flair for storytelling; his narrations were accompanied by flamboyant gestures and hair-raising sound effects, which made his stories better than any fairy tales he could have read us from a book.

We looked forward to those evening story sessions as the high point of the day.

Papa would leave for work in the morning looking fresh and crisp in his suit and tie, with his pencils peeking from his pocket where his handkerchief should have been. He always wore a slouchy felt hat perched on the back of his head. He would return in the evening with his face dark with whiskers, his tie undone, his sleeves rolled up, and looking, in general, as if he had been sleeping in the park all day.

It seems to me in retrospect that he must have worked very hard at his job, though he made it sound at the time as if he were merely having fun. After all, what other fathers got to ride in fire engines and police cars with sirens blaring?

My sisters and I were incorrigible tomboys, I'm afraid. We played baseball in the backyard and cops and robbers in the alleyways around the house. Our knees were perpetually skinned and rough from so much contact with the ground. We dressed in jeans and wrinkled shirts, having no mother to iron them for us, and never realized we were deprived. In fact, it was the happiest time I can remember. Our days were filled with adventure and, in the evenings, we had Papa and his stories. And then, when Nancy was

nine and I was seven and Bettie was only
five, something happened which threatened to
change all this. Papa announced, one day
that he was bringing a friend home to tea. A
lady friend. He made this announcement as he
was leaving for work one morning, tossing it
off as though it were nothing out of the
ordinary, which it most definitely was. And
perhaps we felt the slightest tingle of
apprehension when he suggested that we dust
the living room and bake some cookies for
his guest. We didn't even dust the living
room for Aunt Hilda, who came sometimes on
Sundays and always scolded Papa for the
"state" the house was in.

We did not dust the living room that day
either, as I recall, but we did bake a batch
of chocolate cookies, at which we had become
expert. Papa was diabetic and could eat no
sweets, so we had learned to make our own.
To this day I cringe, when I remember the
condition the kitchen was in when we were
through. Aunt Hilda would have been
apoplectic.

We waited on the front porch for Papa,
as we always did, dressed in our jeans and
rumpled shirts. Bettie always gave a little
shriek when Papa's figure appeared at the
corner under the maple tree, with his jacket
slung over his arm and his newspaper
swinging from his hand. But this day Papa
was late arriving at the corner. In fact, he
did not appear at the corner at all, but
rather came rolling up in a sleek black car
beside a lady in a brown hat like a bird's
nest.

She was pretty in a rather pale and glacial way; I remember thinking that she looked as if she had been carved from ice. She was also very thin, with a body like a sharp stick.

"This is Miss Bevis, girls," he introduced her to us. His tie was still done, and he hadn't even taken off his jacket. He looked almost as fresh as when he'd left that morning, except for the slight darkening of his cheeks.

"How do you do, children?" Miss Bevis asked in a voice dripping of ice water. Then she extended her fingertips for us to touch, and they were even colder.

"Come right on in, Blanche," said Papa with a broad smile. "The girls will get us some tea."

We must have looked stricken, the three of us, for we had never heard Papa call any woman by her first name before, except for Aunt Hilda, of course, and that hardly counted.

"Did you *hear* what he said?" Nancy hissed, when Papa had escorted Miss Bevis through the door. "He called her *Blanche*." She said this in the same way she might have said that he had called her an escaped convict from the state prison.

We served Papa and his guest tea in chipped cups and placed a plate of cookies on the coffee table. Then, at Papa's insistence, we settled restlessly on the couch, watching this strange ritual through saucer eyes.

"Have a cookie, Blanche," said Papa. "The girls are good little bakers."

Miss Bevis lifted a chocolate cookie with her icy fingertips and nibbled at one edge, wrinkling her nose as if expecting it to taste like castor oil. "Yes, quite good," she said, and took a further nibble. I don't know how long it took her to consume that one small cookie, but we watched in fascination as she progressed, rabbit-like, down to the last crumb.

"Miss Bevis works at the newspaper office," said Papa. "She's Mrs. Finley's new secretary."

"What's wrong with his *old* secretary?" Nancy asked archly.

"Old is right," said Papa with a laugh. "Miss Reynolds was nearly as old as the building. She had to retire."

They chatted about business for a while, as we sat watching from the sofa. Miss Bevis seemed to have a whole catalog of complaints against the newspaper company, which she articulated in her high-pitched, rather nasal voice. But Papa didn't seem to mind; he just sat looking at her with a kind of hungry smile, as though he had been trapped on a desert island and she was the first woman he had seen in several years. And it occurs to me now that he probably *was* starved for adult female companionship, with Mama dead and only us three little girls to keep him company.

Suddenly Miss Bevis turned her frigid gaze on us and tried on a brief, pinched smile. "You know," she said in her icy

219

voice, "I would just *love* to see you children in some pretty dresses. Perhaps some organdy or dotted swiss."

"You can't play baseball in a dress," said Nancy flatly.

Strike one against Miss Bevis.

"Ooh," she said, apparently aghast, "baseball is entirely too rough for little girls. It isn't ladylike. You should be playing with dolls and tea sets. *Baseball* is for boys."

Strike two!

Miss Bevis turned back to Papa abruptly, with her arched brows drawn together in a frown of disapproval. "You know, Raymond," she said, "you really should look into dancing lessons for these children. That would make *real* little ladies out of them."

Strike three! She was out.

At the end of that interminable afternoon, when Miss Bevis had finally graced us with her absence, Nancy called a conference in the bedroom.

"That brazen hussy," she exclaimed, "she's only interested in Papa for his money."

"But Papa doesn't have any money," I reminded her, "except for what he makes at the newspaper."

"Well, I don't care," she insisted. "You can tell she's nothing but a gold-digger." Nancy, being the eldest, was allowed to attend Saturday matinees at the Bijou Theater, and so knew all about brazen hussies, gold-diggers and the like.

"We've got to save Papa," she proclaimed, "before Miss Bevis gets him in her *clutches*."

On that point we were all agreed. The thought of having Miss Bevis around was too horrifying for words. She was right out of a fairy tale, it seemed, out of *Cinderella* or *Hansel and Gretel*, the very personification of the wicked stepmother.

And sure enough, a few days later Papa announced that Miss Bevis was once again coming to tea. And once again he asked us to dust the living room and bake some cookies. "It would be nice," he added from the doorway, "if you would wear your Sunday dresses for her. She doesn't like to see little girls in trousers."

Well, that was simply going too far. Such a desperate situation called for a desperate remedy, and another bedroom conference was hastily called.

"I've got an idea," Nancy whispered conspiratorially, even though there was no one around to hear. "We've got to make Miss Bevis wish she'd never come here. We've got to scare her away, before it's too late."

"But how can we do that?" asked Bettie in her little baby's voice.

"It's something I saw in a movie once," said Nancy, her eyes gleaming with intrigue. "It'll make Miss Bevis sorry she ever came here, or Mickey Mantle doesn't know a spit ball from a slider."

That was good enough for me.

And so that afternoon we baked another batch of chocolate cookies - laced with

221

about half-a-pound of pepper. When we took them from the oven, they looked and smelled like any ordinary pan of freshly baked cookies, as plump and soft and tempting.

Out of habit, Bettie reached for one and Nancy slapped her hand. "Are you crazy?" Nancy said. "Do you want to set your mouth on fire? These cookies are for Miss Bevis and Miss Bevis alone."

We donned our Sunday dressed, as Papa had requested, and gave the living room a cursory dusting with a feather duster that was nearly bald. We even washed Bettie's smudged face and combed her hair. Everything must be just right.

Papa and Miss Bevis rolled up in her long black car just after five. We were not watching from the porch, as usual, but were seated demurely on the sofa in the living room. I could see that Papa was pleased to see us so auspiciously decked out in dresses.

Miss Bevis once more extended her icy fingertips for us to touch, then perched, rigidly upright, on the edge of a chair.

"How nice you children look today," she said in frosty tones. "Except there's a spot of dirt you've missed on your chin, dear."

Just as though that were a cue, Nancy lifted the plate of cookies and leaned forward. "Won't you have a cookie, Miss Bevis?" she said sweetly.

"Why, thank you, dear, I believe I will," and Miss Bevis took a large chocolaty cookie still warm from the oven.

We held our breaths. As before, she nibbled around the cookie's edge like a finicky rabbit, and nothing happened. At least, nothing happened for several seconds. Then suddenly Miss Bevis let out a harsh, strangled cry, and when we looked at her she seemed to be weeping. Tears were pouring down her cheeks, which had turned a flaming red, and with both hands she was fanning her face, her cold fish eyes bulging in horror.

"*Eeek!*" she cried, or something very like it, and bolted from the door. In a moment we heard her car roaring from the driveway.

"Well, for goodness' sake," said Papa, "what a strange way to behave."

We never saw her again.

It was a long time before Papa brought another woman home to meet us - over a year, in fact - and in the meantime, he seemed to have forgotten all about Miss Bevis and the effects of the pepper trick.

But we hadn't.

Everything was back to normal, of course. We had Papa all to ourselves once more, we forgot all about dusting the living room and wearing dresses, and Bettie only had to comb her hair on Sundays, when Aunt Hilda was likely to appear.

It was with considerable shock, therefore, that we received the news one Spring morning that Papa was bringing another friend home for tea. Another *lady* friend!

Back to the bedroom, for another conference.

"We'll have to use the pepper trick again," said Nancy in her conspirator's voice. "It's the only way," she added, dramatically.

For some reason I can't recall, we took it for granted that any woman Papa brought home would be as bad as Miss Bevis. Or even worse, perhaps, if such a thing were possible. She was the prototype by which we were to judge all intruders into our domain, sight unseen. We were geared up to defend our territory against all comers, and it was only natural that we should think of the pepper trick again, its having worked so well before.

So certain were we of success, that we didn't bother with non-essentials like dusting or wearing dresses. We went straight to the heart of the matter – which meant baking up another batch of peppered cookies.

We were too excited to wait demurely indoors that day; instead we waited on the porch as usual in our jeans and rumpled blouses. And shortly after five, Papa appeared - not in a sleek black car – but under the maple tree at the corner, as he always did.

And with him was a pretty, dark-haired woman.

"This is Miss Esther Branch, girls," he said when they had reached the porch. His jacket was slung over his arm and his tie was loose; apparently, he had not bothered to stay crisp and fresh for her. "Miss Branch is the nurse in Dr. Wimple's office."

Miss Esther Branch did not look anything at all like Miss Bevis. Where Miss Bevis was sharp Miss Esther Branch was soft and gently rounded, with clear blue eyes that seemed to really twinkle when she smiled, which she was doing now.

"I'm glad to meet you, girls," she said. "I've heard a lot about you from your father. He's very proud of you, you know." Her voice was low and rich and lilting - it reminded me of someone singing.

Inside, we served tea to Papa and Miss Branch and placed a plate of chocolate cookies conspicuously before her. Then we settled nervously on the sofa and waited for the fireworks to begin.

"You must excuse the way the girls are dressed," said Papa, much to our surprise and horror. "I'm afraid they're not too keen on cleaning up or wearing dresses." He was playing right into her hands, in a most traitorous way.

"Oh, but that's perfectly all right, Raymond," said Miss Branch. "It must be very boring to have to sit inside and have tea with stuffy grownups." *How did she know?* "I'll bet they'd rather go outdoors and play some more, before the sun goes down."

Bettie and I both looked at Nancy from the corners of our eyes, only to find her staring at Miss Branch suspiciously. This

225

wasn't at all what we'd expected, what Miss Bevis would have said. Miss Branch was a most peculiar lady. She might almost have been likable in a way, if only she were not out to get Papa in her "clutches", as Nancy had assured us she was.

"Your father tells me you like to play baseball," she said.

"That's right," said Nancy with unspoken challenge in her voice. "I guess you think girls shouldn't *play* baseball, don't you?"

"Oh, quite the contrary," said Miss Branch. "I think it's wonderful that you play baseball, instead of staying cooped up in the house all day with dolls and things. Perhaps you'll let me join you in a game someday."

"*You* play baseball?" we asked, almost in unison.

"Why, I'll have you know I was the best shortstop that Edison Grammar School ever had," said Miss Branch. "And I'll bet you I can still catch a grounder or two," she added with a laugh.

This took us very much off guard. As if inspired by a common urgency, we each looked to the plate of cookies sitting so temptingly before Miss Branch. At any moment she was likely to pick one from the plate and bite into it. I had visions of steam issuing from her ears and mouth, and of her bolting from the room as Miss Bevis had done. Worse, I wasn't at all sure I wanted her to leave.

"Would you believe it? I still have my old baseball glove," Miss Branch was saying, while we sat transfixed, "though it's very old and worn by now, of course. I'll have to bring it over someday and we can have a game of catch."

We gazed at one another then with panic in our eyes. Anyone who owned a well-worn baseball glove must be a kindred spirit and was certainly too good to have peppered cookies served to her. There was only one thing to do, and with only a glance it was agreed upon.

We reached to the plate of cookies and began to stuff them into our mouths, much to Papa's and Miss Branch's amazement. It must have made quite a spectacle, three little girls with bulging cheeks, suddenly and ravenously plucking cookies from a plate.

It was all I could do to keep from yelling. The pepper seemed to burn a hole right through the roof of my mouth and I felt I could have breathed fire at that moment. Tears were streaming down my face, so that I could barely see that Nancy and Bettie were suffering a like distress, their eyes nearly popping from the sockets.

"For heaven's sake, children," Papa exclaimed, "what's going on? You're turning as red as beets."

But we merely continued to gobble up the cookies, shoving them into our mouths and somehow choking them down between gasping for breath. And soon they were nearly gone, with only three left, then only two, then...

But it was too late. Miss Esther Branch picked the final cookie from the plate,

227

before we could snatch it up, and took the tiniest bite of it – just a nibble, really.

"Oh, my goodness, Raymond," she cried, "these cookies are full of pepper! No wonder they're turning red." Then, incredibly, she threw back her head and a cascade of laughter like a waterfall poured out.

We never played the pepper trick again, as you might imagine. For one thing, Miss Branch was the only friend that Papa brought home after that. And sometimes she did play baseball in the yard with us, and go roller skating on the sidewalk before the house... And sometimes at night she'd read us fairy tales in which the villain was a wicked stepmother...

But thanks to Miss Branch, we never had to worry about wicked stepmothers anymore.

18 <u>WHERE DO STORIES COME FROM?</u>

"Where did I come from, Mommy?" asked little Novella.

"I'm not sure what you mean, dear," replied Novella's mother, Novel, who was busy tidying up her pages, smoothing out the dog ears that some inconsiderate reader had left behind. Why on earth would anyone still do this, when it was so easy to make a bookmark out of almost anything, an empty matchbook, for instance, or a discarded junk mail envelope? Some humans just had no business being allowed to handle a respectable book or magazine, even if they *had* purchased it at a second-hand bookstore at half-price. After all, since when did one judge a book by its price, much less its cover? If that were true, then those dreadful paperback romances that were so ubiquitous would have to be given away for nothing.

But such was life in these crass times....

"Do you mean, where do stories, in general, come from?"

"Y... yeah. I guess."

"Well, exactly what kind of stories do you mean, Novella?"

"*You* know, little stories, like me...," insisted Novella.

"Oh, of course," laughed Novel, patting

Novella's little title, "you must mean short stories, don't you, dear?"

"But *I'm* not short!" Novella answered indignantly. "I'm not big like you are yet, but I'm not a *baby* story."

"No, of course not, darling. Why, every day, you're getting longer."

Oh, my! So, it had come to this already? Novel thought, with some consternation — asking these awkward questions, before they were barely old enough to even have a fully developed plot structure yet. No doubt about it, they were constructed much too quickly these days, from idea to outline to first draft.... And Novella's mother blamed it on the modern culture, of course, allowing all that mass-produced junk — not to mention, some new thing called "chick lit" — to sit on the shelves right next to respectable volumes that had very nearly *killed* their authors to create. What must *Madame Bovary* or *Moby Dick* think, when they were shelved in proximity to such unseemly prose? Even *Lolita* was well written, one had to admit, though Novel didn't really approve of *it*, either.

But none of these musings was going to answer Novella's question.

"You see... uh, well... every story has a *Creator*, a... a sacred being to whom we must always give our love and our thanks. For the Creator is all-knowing and all-powerful, and without the Creator we would not exist."

"Does every story have the same Creator?"

230

"Oh, no, my darling," Novel laughed, "there are many different Creators for the thousands and thousands of stories ever created, although some Creators are responsible for more stories than others."

"Were you and I made by the same Creator, Mommy?"

"Of course, and a very wonderful Creator at that, if I do say so."

"But if the Creator made us, then why are you my mommy and not the Creator?"

"Oh, darling, a mommy is a story chosen by the Creator to look after and nurture you until you are big enough and well-written enough to look after yourself. You know how I'm always scolding you for your sloppy grammar or your faulty punctuation? Well... *that* is a mommy's job, Novella. And I will always be here to love and guide you until the day when I'm... well, when I'm out of print."

"But I don't want you to *ever* be out of print, Mommy. I want you to be with me forever and ever."

"Oh, darling, I will be. Just not in the same day I am now. For once a story has been told, it can never be *un*told; it exists in the ether, in the... in the cosmic consciousness, if you will... and, especially, in the memory of anyone who has ever heard or read it. We are much more than just the paper we're printed on, you see; we are our content, our plot and characters and conflict, and those are the things that really matter about us, not whether we still have a shiny dust jacket or pristine pages, despite what the book dealers would have you believe."

"But how do you know which Creator made which story?" asked Novella.

"Well... because... frankly, Novella, some Creators are better than others, and, therefore, their stories are better than the ones by the other Creators."

Novel was beginning to feel quite put out and frustrated by all these questions. "Oh, it's all rather difficult, my dear. You'll understand some day when you're an older story yourself."

"But I like all the stories I play with in the creative writing class, Mommy, no matter who made them. I don't see what difference it makes who their Creator was."

"Well, darling, yes, of course, I know what you mean, but..." Novel had to be very careful here. It would be irresponsible to pass on to Novella any sense of genre discrimination, which was, unfortunately, still so common in the world.

And if the truth be told, as a member of the ruling genre of mainstream fiction, Novel often found it more than a little difficult *not* to feel superior to some of the less... well... *reputable* genres, like American Police Procedurals, for instance, who seemed always to be teeming with low-class criminal types and down-and-out policemen. British murder mysteries at least had some *class* about them, what with their debonair Scotland Yard detectives and cozy Cotswold settings.

232

"We are very fortunate in that our Creator has given us only respectable characters for our stories - even if they *are* tiresomely angst-ridden and neurotic at times."

Novella was thoughtful for a moment. "My main character is a philandering son-of-a-bitch."

Novel turned positively yellowish with shock. "Novella! Where on earth did you learn such disgraceful language?"

"It's what my Creator wrote, Mommy."

"I'll have you know, this is a respectable shelf we reside on, Novella, so please edit yourself before using such words again," Novel said impatiently. "Now then, have I answered your question to your satisfaction, dear? I have some misplaced modifiers to clean up."

Novella gave off a sigh of riffling pages. "Well... to tell you the truth, I feel sort of... confused."

"And why in the *Dickens* is that?"

"Because Daddy told me that we come from some other place called Barnes and Noble."

To which Novel's pages slammed shut.

19 WHAT EVERY WRITER OUGHT TO KNOW: A PRACTICAL GUIDE TO WRITING FICTION

by Lynda Gilmartin (© 1997)

TABLE OF CONTENTS

FOREWORD

Do you think you could write an entire short story without using a single adjective? Not one? Could you give a full sense of what a fictional character is like simply by describing that character's physical surroundings? Do you know how to impart a "sense of place" to all your fiction writing? Do you know how to overcome writer's block?

Whatever your motivation or intent, if you have ever had the urge to try your hand at writing fiction, then I hope – and obviously, I *believe* – that the information and guidance contained in this book will help you set aside your reservations and plunge into the exhilarating, often frustrating but ultimately rewarding experience of fiction writing. Though this booklet is designed primarily for beginning writers, more experienced fiction writers may also find it helpful to be reminded of some of the techniques and nuances of good fiction writing. We writers need to know that we are not alone in our struggles to perfect our writing skills, that there are certain unavoidable pitfalls and the occasional "brick wall" that EVERY writer will sooner or later have to overcome.

The tips and information in this booklet are based on my thirty-plus years of writing fiction, during which time I have seen my stories published in some of the world's top magazines, such as *Ladies' Home Journal*, *Woman's Day*, *Ellery Queen Mystery*

236

Magazine, and others, as well as my tenure as editor for several West Coast publishers and my experience as a creative writing instructor.

This booklet is dedicated to all those die-hard idealists who know in their souls that they MUST write fiction. The impulse to communicate to others through storytelling is a timeless and universal one. And thank heavens it is! Without the dogged determination of all those writers who sit in self-imposed solitude to pursue the craft of writing, the world would be a poorer place by far. Try to imagine for a moment a world in which there was no literature, no wealth of stories from every age and every corner of the world which delight us with their insight, their wit and their perspective on our common plight as human beings. I can only speak for myself, of course, but much of the joy and pleasure I have experienced in my life has come through books, through being carried away on the "wings of words" as utilized by gifted writers.

But, make no bones about it, writing fiction can be either agony or ecstasy, depending upon how amenable one's muse is on any given day. Everyone who has ever tried to write fiction knows the pure agony of staring with growing frustration at a sheet of paper or a computer screen and waiting for the words to come. And waiting, and waiting... I heard this experience described most succinctly once by novelist William

Styron at a writer's conference. Speaking of the difficulties of writing his award-winning novel, *Sophie's Choice,* Styron said that at the end of every eight- or ten-hour writing session, he felt desperately relieved to have just *one* good page of writing, and that to the end of that page he always felt like appending a suicide note!

This is pretty-dramatic testimony to the fact that writing good fiction can be a grueling process, and it is not one to be undertaken by the faint of heart. Indeed, there is something masochistic in ALL creative endeavor, a kind of exposure of the soul that can at times be devastating.

The ecstasy, on the other hand, is when an idea distills itself into words and pages easily, as though the "angel of writing" were directing one's fingers on the keys or paper; when the descriptive passage paints itself upon the page in vivid language, for instance, or when a lovely little alliterative phrase presents itself unforced. When this happens, there is no power on earth that can dissuade the dogged writer from pushing forward into that mysterious, "undiscovered country" of the imagination.

Creative writing can be an intensely satisfying and even therapeutic endeavor, but, contrary to what many people believe – *it is not easy!* I simply cannot count the number of times people have told me, upon learning that I write fiction, that they had often felt that they, too, could write fiction, if they "just had the time." Oh, if only it were that simple! A matter of tossing off engaging stories in spare moments, without any preparation or study, without "paying any dues", as the old-time jazz musicians used to say.

In truth, writing – and especially, *writing well* – is one of the most challenging and difficult endeavors one can embark upon. It will test your patience, your self-esteem and your endurance, both physical and emotional, and all in the service of an exercise for which there are no guaranteed results and no promise of certain reward at the end of the struggle. Indeed, there will be many times when the only reward you will reap for your hours of labor will be the knowledge that *you did it!* You got it off your chest, you put into words the story which would not leave you alone, and now, you're a better, or at least, more experienced writer than when you started.

Whether you intend to write for personal satisfaction or for publication and profit, you need to know at the outset, however, that you will be laying yourself open to two of the most unpleasant experiences a human being can have – criticism and rejection – indignities which even the most renowned and successful writers occasionally must suffer, from editors, readers, and most painfully, themselves. No one escapes it. No one!

Writers, therefore, need to learn early on how to deal with the negative input they will inevitably get from others, whether it comes from family and friends or from editors. One of the best methods of doing this is by forming relationships with other writers with whom you can discuss, not only your work, but the anxieties and obstacles which accompany it. Sharing horror stories as well as successes with other writers is one of the best morale boosters a writer can have. If possible, seek out a writing group in your area or take a creative writing class at your local community college. Or, form your own writing group and solicit members from your circle of friends and acquaintances. Believe me, you are almost surely *not* the only person you know who is interested in writing.

As for rejection – well, that is a given in the writing world. No writer ever lived who did not face rejection at some time or other. Some of the best writers you never heard of are the ones who let it defeat them and make them quit trying. F. Scott Fitzgerald liked to tell the story of having papered his college dorm room with rejection slips from editors before he ever sold a story. But a rejection slip should not be regarded as a definitive comment on your ability, only an assessment of a particular work. Unfortunately, most editors do not have the time, or, in many cases, the inclination to tell you what you did right in a story or novel which they are rejecting, but only that they do not want it. The vast majority of rejection notices are curt and impersonal and, therefore, very deflating to the writer.

Rather than see this as unarguable indictment of your ability, however, you can, believe it or not, use the formal rejection slip as a positive incentive to refocus your long-term objective.

Stop visualizing your name on the *New York Times* Best Seller List for the present and make it your initial goal to receive your first rejection slip that contains a personal comment from the editor. When this happens, it means that editor found something in your work worthy of notice. It is a great step forward, a metaphorical "green light" to keep pursuing your dream.

With that in mind, let us begin.

CHAPTER 1.

BEFORE YOU WRITE A WORD

The English novelist, Somerset Maugham, was once asked if there were any rules for novel writing. "Yes," Maugham replied, "there are three hard and fast rules for writing novels. Unfortunately, no one knows what they are."

While Maugham's observation was restricted to the writing of novels, it might fairly be said to apply to *all* fiction writing, whether long or short form, especially since the advent of something vaguely called "Post-Modernism", which has turned the traditional concept of "good" fiction on its head. But while there are no "hard and fast rules" for fiction, there *are* certain indispensable elements of good creative writing which you will want to be aware of. Unless you are going to write a strictly "experimental" novel or short story – and all good luck to you, if you are – then you will need to get a fix on what makes a novel or short story work, what hooks the reader and then keeps him or her engaged in the unfolding plot. How is character developed? Which point of view works best for a particular story idea? *Et cetera, et cetera.*

And the only way, as far as I am concerned, to understand these qualities and requirements of fiction – until they are second nature to you – is by reading, reading, reading…

That's why I strongly advise, for the beginning writer, an initial period devoted to reading. And I mean READING, READING, READING, until your eyes begin to water, and the words blur on the page. You cannot expect to be good at something you are unfamiliar with, after all – and in the case of fiction writing, naturally that would mean a GREAT DEAL of fiction. It is an undeniable truth that the best instruction in writing good fiction is to READ good fiction. And by good fiction, I do not necessarily mean only the accepted "classics" of great literature, though I highly recommend, at the very least, dipping into these, also: I mean ALL fiction that employs language and imagination in such a way that the reader is taken out of himself or herself, for a period of time, and thrust fully into the world the writer has created. This may include anything from a "hard-boiled" detective novel to one of Jane Austen's genteel depictions of English society at the turn of the nineteenth century.

So, set aside an amount of time in which to immerse yourself totally in the reading of fiction. I recommend personally that you start out by reading a wide range of styles and genres – anything and everything that sounds halfway interesting to you, from a Thomas Hardy novel to a Harlequin Romance. Later, when you have better feel for what works and what doesn't work in fiction, you may begin to concentrate on the type of fiction that most interests you as a writer; that is to say, mainstream, mystery, romance, science fiction, historical, *et cetera*.

Even if your interest is strictly confined to contemporary literature, it is a good idea to read works from a variety of periods and cultures – that is, French, British, Russian, *et cetera* – tasting some of the world's great literary accomplishments. You may not see the necessity in this, but I assure you it is there. Writers need to have a strong cultural and literary background, a wide range of cultural reference points, if you will, in order to acquire the broadest possible perspective on life and the human condition. Otherwise, you run the risk that your writing will be lacking in depth and insight. You will be depriving yourself of the richness of literary form and tradition as developed through the centuries all over the world.

In my own, long writing career, I have always found my greatest inspiration and impetus in reading the works of other writers, writers whose mastery of the various forms of fiction so capture my imagination that I am filled with the burning desire to equal their achievements. "I want to write that well!" my mind begins to shout, and soon, I am hitting the keyboard with renewed energy and determination.

Reading for Technique

It is important for an aspiring writer to learn to read with a writer's eye and ear, which is different from reading simply for enjoyment or information. This means being aware of *technique* as well as of content as you read. It means slowing down your reading at times, so that you can literally analyze the writing, taking note of the diction, grammatical constructions, figurative language, punctuation and other elements of the writer's style. What "devices" does the writer employ, to achieve a particular effect? How does he or she handle transitions from one scene or focus to another? How is dialogue constructed so that it flows smoothly and has the sound of real speech? And what is the relationship between the writer and the reader, and does it enhance the writing or detract from it?

You may not be able to grasp the finer points of any writer's style in one reading, or even several. You may, in fact, need to reread certain passages again and again before you begin to "see" how the writer *constructed* it. In fact, it is helpful to think of a work of fiction, or any passage of it, as if it were a building which has been constructed, from the foundation up, of various materials. As you read, you can "deconstruct" the writing to find out what those are, and how they are used in relationship to one another. "Deconstruction", by the way, is a term currently popular in literary criticism, but

245

I am not using it here in quite the same sense, which is complicated and somewhat controversial.

When I ask that you "deconstruct" a passage of writing, I intend only that you examine the constituent parts and how they are used in a phrase, sentence, or paragraph to achieve a desired effect.

Before leaving this subject, I would add that it is also important to familiarize yourself with current standards in the use of punctuation marks, which have changed considerably over the past twenty or thirty years, and this is best done by paying close attention to the use of punctuation in contemporary writings. You may not feel that it is necessary for you, the writer, to concern yourself overmuch with the proper use of punctuation – that it is the job of an editor to correct your mistakes in that area – but this is underestimating, I believe, the important role that punctuation plays in conveying meaning and emotion, and in promoting clarity of thought.

The accepted rules of punctuation have been greatly modified in recent years. Editors and writers these days seem to adhere to the philosophy that less is more, regarding punctuation, sometimes to the point of making writing, in my opinion, almost incomprehensible. But there is a happy medium, a sensible standard for the use of punctuation to facilitate meaning and intent, without the plethora of rules which,

246

in former times, sometimes threatened to submerge the writing in a sea of commas and semicolons.

Note: Before we leave the subject of reading, I would issue a word of caution, with respect to reading the works of other writers. Once you have begun actual work on your own writing project, be careful what you read while your work is in progress. As I have found to my sorrow on more than one occasion, it is very easy to be influenced by the powerful writing of a skilled and experienced author. You may find your own story veering off into directions you hadn't intended. OR, you may begin to compare your writing unfavorably to that in the work you are reading and become discouraged. Fending off those feelings of self-doubt and insecurity is one of the writer's most urgent and important tasks.

So, reading the genuinely good works of literature – the writers who will inspire you to do better work yourself – should be relegated to those periods between writing projects. If you are like me, you cannot ever swear off reading altogether. Nor should you. I find that what works best for me is to read simple escapist literature when I am deeply involved in my own writing project, works that do not make too great an impression on my mind nor stir my writer's sensibilities overmuch. You may even think of these times as a good excuse to indulge in all the glitzy, "trash" fiction that you wouldn't ordinarily seek out.

CHAPTER 2.

GETTING DOWN TO WORK

And now to the work at hand. When the light bulb in your head suddenly switches on, and you are "electrified" by an absolutely smashing idea for a story or novel, the impulse is to head straight for the keyboard and begin to write. Okay. So, do that, if you must. Put down a few experimental sentences, a possible opening paragraph, even, if that will help give the idea some validity and concreteness in your mind. (One of the great fears of writers is that their ideas will dissipate before they're fully born.) Then, step back and let the story, and all of its elements, begin to germinate in your consciousness. Very rarely – *if ever* – does a story idea does a story idea occur full-blown, even to the most experienced writer. No one – not even the most successful and prolific author – can expect to simply sit down one day and begin writing a work of fiction. There must be PREPARATION, a period devoted to thought and planning, regarding plot structure, setting, characterization, point of view, *et cetera*.

You will also want to decide on a *focus* for your story. This means narrowing your vision to concentrate on a particular element or thread of the many plot possibilities your story idea may suggest. During the Italian Renaissance, artists such as Leonardo da Vinci used a contraption called the *camera obscura*, which was a box with a small square slot cut out on facing sides and perfectly aligned with one another. Looking through these square slots at the scene to be painted gave the artist a well-defined *perspective* on the scene within a circumscribed space. This is very much the same thing as *focus* in writing; it means limiting your "scene" but describing it in depth and detail.

Let's say you want to write a novel based on the American Civil War. Obviously, this is far too broad a subject to cover in any work of fiction. Therefore, you must decide on a specific aspect of the war which interests you, and concentrate on bringing to life, as fully as possible, the characters and events within this narrower scope. The most famous Civil War novel ever written, for example, Margaret Mitchell's *Gone with the Wind*, focuses on the effects of the war on a small group of people, living in Atlanta just before General Sherman's catastrophic march through the city. Limiting her focus in this way allowed Mitchell to give her story the vividness and immediacy which has placed it among the classics of American literature.

Another note of caution here. I have learned from my own experience, and that of many other writers, that it can be exceedingly dangerous to discuss your story ideas with others, before your project is well underway, until that point in the writing when you are well and truly committed, intellectually and emotionally, to the project. It is only natural to want feedback from others, to have someone else confirm for you that your story concept is a valid one. Too often, however, in discussing story ideas with others, the writer will begin to feel his or her drive to follow-through on the idea dissipating. It's almost as though it is enough to have expressed the idea verbally to someone else, and the original desire to see the concept in completed form is somehow diminished. You may not think this could happen to you, but if you discuss your story ideas too freely with others, you could be in for a most unpleasant surprise.

The other, and equally disastrous, consequence of discussing story ideas results from the normal human impulse to offer some "input" on the projects of others. Getting "input" from a sympathetic friend or colleague may *sound* like a good idea, but, trust me, usually it is not. After all, it is nearly impossible to convey in conversation the full scope and depth of your idea, all the nuances and shading of the story as it has been simmering in your consciousness. Your listener is hearing merely a capsule version of a plot and will probably not be able to grasp the full potential of your story idea. And listening to well-intended advice, based on an incomplete understanding of your intentions for your story, can only serve to shake your confidence and undermine your faith in your work. The egos of writers are notoriously fragile - for very good reason - and need all the protection and nurturing possible. (There are exceptions, of course - the strutting and egomaniacal writers who think they are God's own gift to the literary world, but they form a small minority of writers. The rest of us live with constant uncertainty and a fair degree of anguish concerning the worth of our own writing.)

Deciding on a Point of View

One of the most crucial decisions you must make before beginning work on your project is which point of view you will employ. From whose perspective is the story to be told; that is, who is telling the story, and what degree of knowledge and insight does this unseen narrator have into the minds of the other characters?

Points of view may be either first- or third-person. In first-person POV, the story is told by a narrator who may either be an objective observer of the events or a participant in them. This narrator can only communicate his or her own thoughts and feelings about the unfolding events and acts as a recorder of the actions of the other characters. In the first instance, the narrative might begin thusly: "I had not seen Treadway since the war and was surprised when I learned that he was running for Parliament." In this case, the narrator is to be a first-person observer of the events; he is a non-participating character in the story, recording and, perhaps, commenting upon the actions of the other characters. OR, it may begin, "In the summer of 1982, I decided, against all rational objections to the contrary, to run for Parliament." In this case, the narrator is Treadway himself, who is to be an active participant in the unfolding story, perhaps even its central character.

Third-person POVs fall into three categories; omniscient, selective omniscient and objective. In omniscient POV, the narrator is a non-participating observer who can see into the minds and hearts, so to speak, of all the characters of the story, so that the events of the story are seen from a plural number of overlapping perspectives. An omniscient POV might take the following forms: "Jonathan was reluctant to confess the depth of his feelings for Marcia, who took his silence for rejection. In desolation she turned to Wilfred, who offered solace with a patience he hoped would win him her affections." Here we are given insight into the mental processes of three different characters, and the same will hold true for all the characters of the story.

In selective omniscient, the outside narrator sees into the mind of one, or of a selected few, of the characters; other characters are viewed strictly objectively and only their words and actions are recorded. This is a commonly used point of view; it circumscribes the narration in a way which allows the writer to concentrate upon specific characters.

And lastly, in the third-person objective, the outside narrator cannot see into the minds of the characters, but only records what is happening from an objective viewpoint. In such cases, we can only surmise the thoughts and feelings of the characters from their actions and reactions and from their speech.

Only you, as a writer, can decide from which point of view to tell your story. You may even have to experiment with various POVs to discover the one which feels most comfortable to you and which will tell your story best. Some stories will lend themselves more easily to the first-person format, for instance, which, by its nature, has a more personal tone; it has the character of a memoir-type of narration and is a more intimate and immediate way of telling a story. Some writers may find that this also makes the overall project more *manageable* for them, as they do not have to explore the psychological processes of any character other than the narrator.

Third person omniscient or selective, on the other hand, allows the writer more freedom to explore what is going on in the minds of various characters, which may lend the story a greater depth and color as far as the characterizations and the tone of the story are concerned. Most romance novels and, of necessity, psychological thrillers are written in this POV, as well as much mainstream fiction. (For an exemplary instance of the third person omniscient point of view at its best, read almost any of British writer Ruth Rendell's masterful explorations of the human psyche.) Third person objective, on the other hand, is a more *reportorial* format and works well for stories in which the action of the story is more important than the underlying psychology of the characters. It moves the story along at a faster pace and gives precedence to the *events* of the story, rather than to the characters. Police procedurals and other types of murder mysteries, westerns, action/adventure stories, et cetera, often employ this point of view to good effect.

Give careful consideration, to the point of view you will take in your own work, before getting too far into it. It can be a deciding factor in whether your story idea becomes a workable project and is told to best effect.

CHAPTER 3.

PLAYING GOD

In a way, writers get to "play God." Not only do they get to create an entire world out of nothing but the seeds of their imaginations, they get to control the flow of events and the course of their characters' lives, as well, for good or ill, better or worse. The characters in your story can only do and be what you allow them to. This kind of "omnipotence" in regard to the fictional lives of one's characters is heady stuff to the inexperienced writer and may seem to have no drawbacks.

But this is where insight, judgment and discipline come into play in the writer's craft. In truth, in *good* fiction, the writer DOES NOT have indiscriminate control over what happens to his or her characters – not if he or she wants the story to be believable. As most experienced fiction writers will tell you, once you have established a set of fully drawn and *believable* characters in a specific environment, those characters will begin to take on a life and a will of their own – just as if they were real human beings, living real lives. Even a writer as renowned as William Faulkner once complained that the characters he created for his novels seemed to have minds of their own. And this is where the writer must stop "playing God" and begin to be the wise parent to his or her creation, subtly molding and directing the story's characters to be and do what is right for the story.

If you have fully developed your story idea and constructed the foundation of a feasible and engaging plot, you will find, as you get further and further into your story, that it at times seems to want to take unexpected twists and turns, ones you hadn't foreseen when you began the project. You may even, at times, feel as though a particular character is pulling you off the main track of your story, as new and interesting possibilities for that character occur to you. This is just what happens in real life, after all, as "real" human beings act out of impulses and motivations they may not even be conscious of. And this is where the writer must exercise something like parental control, allowing his or her characters to behave and react in a realistic fashion without sabotaging the plot or their own roles in it. It means not following every impulse to allow your characters to wander down a path which *you* may find interesting, but which may detract from your plot.

Fiction writers, after all, tend to become deeply attached to the characters they create and often regard them almost as their "children." But as with real-life children, they must not be indulged in every whim and fancy of the moment; some restraint must be exercised in allowing characters to expand beyond the requirements of the story. You, as the writer, must keep alert to the danger of letting a character(s) stray from the general plot outline you have established.

Writers should also beware of following too freely on the trail of various sub-plots and "stories within a story," no matter how interesting or appealing they may seem to you at the time. Always keep in mind the basic blueprint for your story as you have carefully designed it and adhere to as streamlined a plan as possible for telling that story. Otherwise, you may find yourself at some point writing an entirely different story from the one you intended.

(As long as we are on the subject, just let me say that asides and diversions along the way are fine, even desirable at times, so long as they do not detract from the original purpose and focus on your plot. For, while Thomas Hardy, writing in the late nineteenth century, may have been able to get away with a ten-page discussion of the history of stone masonry in England, the contemporary reader rarely has the patience – or, in many cases, the attention span – for rambling asides which do nothing to advance the plot. Keep all such asides as brief, cogent, and interesting as possible, and do not stray so far away from the main action of the story that the reader will not be able to effortlessly *re-engage* in the plot. Otherwise, you may lose the momentum of your story – and your reader, as well.)

The goal, therefore, is to maintain a reasonable control over your characters and their actions, while at the same time allowing them to develop into fully realized, three-dimensional entities. Toward this end, it is a good idea, before you begin your first draft, to write a "thumbnail" sketch of your major characters, to try to develop them, as fully as possible, as viable and believable human beings. This means not only imagining them as they exist in your story, but as they would exist in "real" life. What factors and influences have molded them and brought them to the particular time and place and circumstance where your story begins? What are their personal traits and quirks, their likes and dislikes, their strengths and weaknesses? How will they likely react to the unfolding situation in your plot? It will not be as difficult as you might think to *realize* a fully-fleshed character. Most of the characters that fiction writers create are based at least partially on, or are composites of, real people they know or have known in their own lives. But be careful in doing this; don't choose a jumble of contradictory traits for your character, selected randomly from the most interesting or unusual people you know.

One very effective way of establishing "character," for instance, is through describing the character's personal surroundings. Our environment, our homes and offices, the life they give us (assuming we have the power to control those surroundings), begin to reflect us after a measure of time, as we leave the marks of our personal lives – the quirks and traits of our individual personalities – on that environment. Think of the home of someone you know fairly-well. Are there photographs and mementoes of family and loved ones in evidence? Or is there a conspicuous absence of the obvious signs of close personal relationships on show? Is there a cozy disorder about the rooms, as though the occupants feel comfortable and at ease in the home? Or do the rooms have a stark, unlived-in look, indicative that the occupants regard the premises as a temporary accommodation and not a real home? Does the home contain any books, and if so, how many, and of what kind? Are the rooms light and airy, or dark and closed-in, as though better to hide from the outside world in?

There are the "nuances" of environment which tell us so much about human beings, and they are also the tools the fiction writer employs to explore and define character and mood.

The following excerpt from *Madame Bovary,* published in 1856, provides an excellent example of personal environment and what it may tell about the characters of a story. In it, author Gustave Flaubert is describing the country home of Dr. Charles Bovary:

> The brick front of the house was flush with the street, or rather the road. Behind the door hung a coat with a short cape, a bridle and a black leather cap, and on the floor in one corner lay a pair of gaiters still caked with mud. To the right was the "parlor," which was actually a living room and dining room combined. The canary-yellow wallpaper, embellished at the top by a border of pale flowers, rippled everywhere over its loose cloth backing; white calico curtains edged with red braid overlapped

259

each other down the length of the windows, and on the narrow mantelpiece a clock adorned with a bust of Hippocrates stood majestically between two silver-plated candlesticks with oval glass shades. Across the hall was Charles' office. It was a small room, no more than six paces wide, with a table, three simple chairs and an office armchair. The six shelves of the fir bookcase were filled almost entirely by a set of the *Dictionary of the Medical Sciences* whose pages were uncut, but whose bindings had suffered in the process of being bought and sold by a long succession of different owners. The smell of cooking sauces came through the walls during consultations, and from the kitchen one could hear the patients coughing and giving descriptions of their symptoms.

This writing may seem strangely formal to you if you are unused to the style of nineteenth-century literature. But reread it, paying closer attention this time, and ask yourself what you now know about the character and circumstances of Dr. Bovary, the resident of the house in the excerpt. Is he a wealthy, cultured man, a member of the upper class of French society? Is he a man of intellectual depth, a member of the intelligentsia? Is he a man of leisure?

No, he is none of these things. And just how do we know this from reading this one paragraph about his home? Well, for one thing, the house is obviously small and cramped, the living and dining areas combined in one room, the so-called "parlor," in which the cheap wallpaper is buckling over its backing. The windows are adorned with simple calico curtains, certainly not what one would expect to find in the home of an upper-class "gentleman." The candlesticks on the mantelpiece are merely silver-*plated*, rather than made of pure silver. And so on, and so on...

Yet another interesting observation we may make about Dr. Bovary from this brief passage is that he is probably not a man of great intellectual depth or learning. The only books in the bookcase are a set of medical dictionaries with fraying bindings and uncut pages. In other words, the books are second-hand, and Dr. Bovary has never even read them; they are only for show.

And finally, there is one last bit of information we may infer about Dr. Bovary from this short excerpt. Remember the "Gaiters," or overshoes, standing in a corner by the door? They are still caked with mud, as though the good doctor expected to be called out again at any moment to attend to a patient. He has learned from experience that there is little point in cleaning the gaiters each time he returns to his home, when he may be trudging out into the muddy streets of the village again at a moment's notice. This tells us, in a very subtle but effective way, that Dr. Bovary, while perhaps not the most cultured or intellectual of men, is a conscientious physician, placing the needs of his patients above any mere social nicety.

This is quite a lot to learn about someone in just one paragraph, you'll probably agree. But Flaubert didn't *tell* you these interesting tidbits about Bovary's character and circumstances. In fact, he never directly alluded to Bovary at all in the passage. Instead, he SHOWED YOU, through a detailed and authentic-sounding description of Bovary's immediate environment, what kind of man, personally as well as professionally, the doctor is.

This is exactly the sort of feat the best fiction writers pull off as a matter of course. It gives their writing both subtlety and power. It AUTHENTICATES their characters by placing them in believable contexts and letting us see them in the natural environments in which they live and move.

Remember! The goal is consistency of character and personality – to make sure your characters seem like REAL people. It would not seem believable, for example, to have a character who is a devoted family man and responsible citizen, suddenly become a womanizing, free-wheeling hedonist... UNLESS you show what forces and influences were at work to bring about such a drastic transformation.

Put simply, BELIEVABILITY is always the goal in characterization.

CHAPTER 4.

<u>LOCATION, LOCATION, LOCATION</u>

If our environment reflects us and our individuality, we also reflect our environment. The best fiction almost always has a "sense of place", a unique setting in which the characters move and act and feel, whether it is the French countryside of Flaubert's *Bovary*, the fictional Mars of Ray Bradbury's *Martian Chronicles* or the Louisiana bayou setting of contemporary mystery writer James Lee Burke. Setting may even exert a direct influence on the unfolding of the plot, as it does in Jack London's Alaskan novels and stories, in which the characters are pitted against the indomitable forces of a harsh and unforgiving landscape. In such works of fiction, the setting almost becomes a non-human *character* in the story, exerting influences over the plot much in the way a human character might.

Real Estate professionals like to say that there are three important factors in selling real estate, and those three are LOCATION, LOCATION, LOCATION. If we simply change the word "location" to "setting" we writers might almost adopt this dictum for our own. The setting of any story should ring with authenticity, whether you are placing your story in a real setting or creating one solely out of your imagination. Consider the following passage from Mark Twain's *Huckleberry Finn*, in which Huck is describing what it is like to be on a raft in the middle of the Mississippi at night:

> Sometimes we'd have that whole river all to ourselves for the longest time. Yonder was the banks and the islands, across the water; and maybe a spark – which was a candle in a cabin window – and sometimes on the water you could see a spark or two – on a raft or a scow, you know, and maybe you could hear a fiddle or a song coming over from one of them crafts. It's lovely to live on a raft...
>
> Once or twice of a night we could see a steamboat slipping along in the dark, and now and then she would belch a whole world of sparks up out of her chimbleys, and they would rain down in the river and look awful pretty; then she would turn a corner and her lights would wink out and her pow-wow shut off and leave the river still again; and by-and-by her waves would get to us, a long time after she was gone, and joggle the raft a bit, and after that you wouldn't hear nothing for you couldn't tell how long, except maybe frogs or something.

As you read this passage, can you imagine yourself on a makeshift raft in the middle of the mighty Mississippi River as night is falling? Can you sense the quietness and calm, and then the sudden interruption of

264

the stillness as a steamboat passes by, disgorging a spray of fiery sparks into the air? Can you feel the gentle rocking of the small raft in the wake of the chugging steamboat?

If you cannot, then read the passage again, attentively, and you will experience the power of a great writer to transport us far, far away from where we are through the magic of his writing. Of course, Twain was writing of something with which he was very familiar - the Mississippi River, on which he had traveled as a river pilot.

SO, fully know your setting first - know the geographical terrain, the architecture, the ambience - as well as you know your own hometown, your own home, your own bedroom... If you are creating a setting from scratch - that is, one that does not exist in actuality - then, try to imagine it in as much detail as possible. *Create* it in your mind, furnish it and live in it a while, until it becomes so familiar to you, that you almost begin to believe that it really exists somewhere.

One of the most famous imaginary settings ever created is found in the South American author Gabriel Garcia Marquez's *One Hundred Years of Solitude*. In this amazing novel, Marquez has fabricated the lush, tropical city of Macondo, which sits in the middle of a South American mountain jungle much like those found in his native Colombia. The city has the quality of a vivid dream in which bizarre and beautiful things happen at every turn. But Marquez has so fully realized Macondo that by the end of the book, we are half convinced that it has a physical existence.

If you are placing your story in an actual setting, be sure it is one with which you are fairly-familiar and can describe accurately enough to imbue your story with a "sense of place." Don't place your story or novel in Venice, Italy, for example, if you have never set eyes on the place. While it *is* possible to research a setting so thoroughly that you may be able to provide a superficial description of it, this is a very tricky business that even some very experienced writers could not pull off. If you do try this, more than likely your descriptive passages will have a travel-brochure feel; you will not be able to impart the feel and smell and sounds of Venice, for instance, as intimately as if you had spent time there actually.

The mistake some inexperienced writers make is in thinking that they *must* give their stories some exotic locale, in order to capture the reader's interest. This is simply not true, however. Even the most-humble locale can be made to throb with life, as indeed, it almost surely *does* throb with life, beneath the surface in reality. If the only place you are familiar with is your own hometown, then, by all means, think of making this your setting – or at least, some fictionalized version of it. After all, you are an authority on this particular setting,

266

and should be able to make it come to life for your readers. You know the way the air feels at sunset, or sunrise; how the seasons change the landscape, for better or worse; how welcoming, or not, the faces of the houses are, *et cetera*... Don't undervalue or misjudge even the simplest of settings. Everywhere there is life, there is something fascinating going on, you can be sure.

Perhaps I can illustrate what I mean with the following story. I once had a brief stay in the hospital where my brother-in-law was recovering from surgery. To fend off boredom, I kept a daily journal in which I recorded everything I saw and heard and experienced in that place, from the décor of the rooms to the distinctive sounds of a hospital at night. I noted the cheap prints of Parisian street scenes which adorned the walls, the quaint "inspirational" messages on the daily menus, the clatter of the ice machine across the hall...

When I later showed this journal to my brother-in-law, he was simply amazed. How had I managed to see and hear so much that he had missed in this place, he wanted to know. The simple answer would have been that I'm a writer, and I'm curious. About *everything*.

The key is to become an acute and non-judgmental observer of your surroundings and the people in it. I firmly believe that in every writer worth his or her salt there lurks an incurable eavesdropper, someone who is infinitely curious about life and,

267

especially, about human beings and their machinations.

The bottom line in conveying a sense of place, then, is that you must be able to take your readers with you to whatever destination you are utilizing for your story; you must be able to make them feel as if they have truly been there, if only in imagination. You can only do this by careful attention to detail and by imparting a true "sense" of the flavor and feel of your setting.

CHAPTER 5.

HE SAID/SHE SAID

One of the most difficult struggles I had as a beginning writer was in learning to write convincing dialogue. This element of fiction writing is a double-edged sword. Not only must your dialogue sound as if real people might have spoken it, the form in which you convey who said what must be unobtrusive, must flow so naturally that the reader will feel as if he or she is actually *hearing* the dialogue, not reading it. This is what I call "the he said/she said dilemma."

To illustrate what I mean by this, I have written two different versions of a simple passage of dialogue involving three speakers. The first version should show you what problems a writer may run into when faced with the "he said/she said dilemma."

Let us imagine three people, two men and one woman, in a small boat.

"Do you think the fish will bite tonight?" Melina said.

"They will when the wind dies down," said Nikos. "You must be patient."

"We shouldn't have come out at all on such a gusty night," Stavros said. "I can feel a storm brewing."

"You imagine things!" said Nikos. "What kind of fisherman fears a little wind?"

"A fisherman who wants to live to fish another day," said Melina.

"I agree," said Stavros. "I don't like the looks of that sky at all."

"I tell you, I'm not going in until I've caught a fish for my dinner," said Stavros.

Not very interesting, is it? Of course, the dialogue is not connected to any story, but is for illustrative purposes only, and therefore: we are in the dark as to the context. But do you see what I mean?

All these "*He said*s" and "*She said*s" have become quite jarring; they constantly *stop* the flow of the dialogue, making us so conscious of the writing that the actual speech sounds contrived. But what to do? How is it possible to convey who is saying what, without this incessant repetition of "he said/she said"? Well, let's try this again and see if there is another, and better, way:

269

"Do you think the fish will bite tonight?" Melina asked.

Nikos shrugged. "They will when the wind dies down. You must be patient."

"We shouldn't have come out at all, on such a gusty night," Stavros muttered, from his corner of the boat. "I can feel a storm brewing."

The other man turned to him with a frown of disdain. "You imagine things! What kind of fisherman fears a little wind?"

"A fisherman who wants to live to fish another day," came the curt reply.

Melina followed Stavros' gaze to the dark clouds on the horizon. "Perhaps we should turn back and head for shore."

"I agree," said Stavros. "I don't like the looks of that sky at all."

But their companion was not to be so easily dissuaded from his quest. "I tell you I'm not going in until I've caught a fish for my dinner!"

His eyes never wavering from the line of lowering clouds in the distance, Stavros spoke with ominous portent. "When that storm blows up and overturns the boat, the fish will be having *you* for dinner, my friend."

This probably sounds a little better.

At least we have dispensed with the constant repetition of "he said/she said", and in the process, given the writing a nicer flow. We have also added a little flavor to the passage, have "filled it out," so to speak, so that we get a fuller and more complete picture of the scene and what is transpiring.

Do you see what I did differently, the technique that makes this version read more smoothly and more interestingly than the first? It's really very simple. Immediately preceding some lines of dialogue, I have added a brief descriptive comment on the speaker, as in "Nikos shrugged" in the second paragraph, which points directly to the speaker of the lines which follow. This is all the indication needed as to who is speaking this segment of dialogue and dispenses altogether with any form of "he said/she said."

Notice that I have used this same type of comment in paragraphs four, six, and eight. This type of commentary on the speaker also enriches the writing, painting the scene and the reactions of the characters in more detail.

If there are only two characters involved in the dialogue, the solution is even simpler, as illustrated in the following example:

"When did you last see your husband, Mrs. Cosgrove?" asked Inspector Dingle.

"Why, at dinner last night. We dined just after eight, and then Nigel retired to his study for the evening, as usual."

"Did you notice anything different in his manner, that he seemed worried or anxious for some reason?"

"Just what are you suggesting, Inspector?"

Dingle's gaze fell to Mrs. Cosgrove's hands, which were held tightly clenched in her lap. "I'm not suggesting anything, Madam. I'm just trying to get at the truth."

Here we have only indicated the speaker one time, in the first sentence; after that, it is pretty clear, from the dialogue itself, who is speaking. This has the advantage of moving the dialogue forward in real time; it builds momentum toward the object or outcome of the conversation. This format works best for relatively brief passages of dialogue, however. In longer passages, you may need to insert an occasional reminder of who is speaking, to avoid confusion on the reader's part, even when there are only two speakers. And when there are three or more speakers, this type of format should be attempted only with great care and be limited to a few segments of dialogue for each character.

Of course, there is much more to writing good dialogue than simply the mechanics of who said what. All dialogue should serve some

272

purpose, whether it is in illuminating character, establishing mood or furthering the plot. It is usually not a good idea to just *fill up space* with dialogue that bears no immediate relationship to the story, no matter how witty or profound you may believe it to be. If you have a particular message or a philosophy to propound, do it within the context of the story and not in extraneous sermonizing. Let your philosophy and attitude toward life be revealed in the story itself, through the actions of your characters and through the consequences of those actions and leave the sermonizing to the preachers and politicians.

Good dialogue will not necessarily *announce* its intent or purpose, however. Indeed, some of the best dialogue may sound deceptively simple, even inconsequential, when taken out of context. If you have a scene in which two women meet on the street and strike up a conversation, for instance, that conversation may *seem* ordinary, it may not seem to exert a direct influence on the plot, but through the nuances of their speech, their responses to each other and their physical attitudes, we may learn quite a lot about the characters of the women, their relationship to each other and their hidden motivations. On close examination, we may even discern in their speech subtle clues regarding the unfolding of the plot. If, for example, one woman's responses are given in a somewhat more formal tone than another's, we might surmise displeasure on her part, a feeling of superiority or even subtle hostility.

This sort of dialogue is building toward an *effect*; it is moving the story forward by revealing to us what the characters are like in unguarded, undramatic moments, so that they become real to us as human beings and not merely as props to a plot.

But how do we make fictional dialogue sound *real*? The simplest answer is that we do this by paying close attention to how people speak in actual life. After all, we want our characters to *talk* to one another, not give speeches. We want them to sound as though they are saying what they would say in real life, not merely what we have *written* for them to say. This does not mean that you will want to include every "hum," "ah," "you know" and "like" that we hear so much in speech patterns today. This is carrying realism a little too far and is almost guaranteed to irritate your reader. Of course, if you are deliberately trying to show that your character is nervous, is stammering in confusion or has some type of speech defect – and if you are, I advise you to utilize this effect very sparingly – you may need or want to include a certain amount of "hemming and hawing" in your dialogue. (I believe one of the strangest things some writers do is have their characters say "er," at the beginning of a sentence to denote uncertainty or reticence. Have you *ever* heard someone say "er" in real life?) Otherwise, sift through the extraneous

274

affectations and "tics" of speech and get to the heart of the matter – what and how people actually communicate.

There are those lucky writers who find that writing good dialogue comes naturally and is no problem, and I envy them. For the rest of us, writing good dialogue – dialogue that has the sound of real speech and that enhances the story – may be a matter of relentless trial and error. There is not much you can do about that but keep trying, keep listening attentively to how people speak, and study how dialogue is done by the best writers.

CHAPTER 6.
EXERCISING YOUR WRITING "MUSCLE"

Just as athletes need to exercise their bodies to stay in top physical condition, so writers need to exercise to keep their writing "muscle" fit. The best way to do this, of course, is to write every day, to set yourself a goal and do your best to reach it, day in and day out.

Science- fiction writer Ray Bradbury likes to say that no one should call himself a writer who does not write at least 1,000 words a day. Though this may seem to be overstating it somewhat, for the majority of us, who feel grateful to have written four or five hundred words of decent prose each day, Bradbury's point is well taken. Flow and momentum in your writing can only be maintained by keeping to a regular writing routine.

This is easy enough to do when you are in the middle of a writing project that is going well, and you feel that you are making steady progress toward completion. But what about those times between projects, when you have no specific daily goal to try for? Should you simply lay off writing altogether, for a period of time, until you are ready to begin a new work?

Not necessarily. In fact, laying off for too long can have a detrimental effect on your writing when you do begin to work consistently again. But what can you do to keep your writing "muscle" fit during periods between projects? One answer is that you can do some simple writing exercises. Not only will this keep you writing but it may teach you some valuable lessons, about language and technique, in the process. These exercises may consist of nothing more than writing long, discursive letters to distant friends or relatives (and won't they be shocked to receive them?), writing a "letter to the editor" on some topic about which you feel strongly, putting into words your long-range plans for your life and work, *et cetera*. And I would like to humbly offer another, and somewhat more specific exercise for you to try.

I want you to read the following short-short story, paying very close attention to the way in which it is written:

"Perspective"

He had tumbled from a leaf made slippery by the rain. Riding on a raindrop, he plummeted into a void which seemed to have no end. He lay now on his back, his legs thrusting skyward, flailing against emptiness and space. He had never seen the sky before; his universe consisted of the clumps of earth and blades of grass through which he crawled in search of food. In his amazement, he forgot to struggle but lay motionless a moment, staring into the vastness over him. He had never imagined so much color in the world, so much shape and space and depth; there were dimensions he had never dreamed of. To see it now filled him with both fear and exultation, and he felt that all the moments of his existence had led him to this glimpse of sky.

Suddenly a shadow appeared, a blot of darkness descending inexorably upon him from above, obliterating the undersides of leaves and wisps of cloud, and sunlight. In his mind he cried out, pleading for time in which to glimpse the wonder of it all. But it was futile. He heard the crunch of footsteps on the ground – the sound of his world exploding, surely! – and he felt himself pressed back into the dirt, enveloped and diffused into the earth from which he'd come.

But he had no regrets... for he had seen the sky."

(*Ed. Note: *Yes, you've seen this one before!*)

Well, what do you think? What is peculiar about this story, other than the fact that it is about the plight of an insect falling to his doom from a leaf? Does the writing have a strange sound and quality? It probably does, for there is an important element of language which is missing. If you have not already guessed what it is, then read the story again and see if you can figure out what makes the story sound so different from ordinary writing.

What is different, of course, is that the story is written entirely without adjectives. That's right! There is not a single adjective throughout the story. Granted, it may not seem like a great story, at first, but it does, I think, communicate what is happening, and to whom.

When I was first given the assignment in a writing class to write a short story without using any adjectives, I wondered if such a thing could be done. Accomplishing the feat stretched my writing "muscle" in a way few writing projects have ever done. It meant I had to delve deep into my writer's repertoire and use all the ingenuity I was capable of summoning, to communicate clearly and effectively without the help of any descriptive or modifying words.

This is the type of exercise which should help you "keep in shape" during those periods when you are not engaged in a work in progress. Try an exercise of this type, writing a short story without using any adjectives, or common names, or place descriptions or the like. It will truly test your ingenuity and give you a new *perspective* on the uses and forms of language.

CHAPTER 7.

WHEN THE WORDS WON'T COME

There comes a time in every writer's life when the words simply won't come, when the creative juices not only stop flowing but seem to have evaporated altogether. Many jokes are made about writer's block, but in truth, it is one of the most painful and debilitating setbacks a committed writer can experience, as captured with agonizing brilliance by Joel and Ethan Coen, in their script for the 1991 movie, *Barton Fink*. Writer's block – and especially, *prolonged* writer's block – can wreak such havoc with a writer's drive and confidence that he or she may literally never write again. But inasmuch as writer's block generally does not destroy *the urge* to write, but only the ability to do so, this means that, in extreme cases, it can truly be a life-altering event.

Before it reaches this point, however, there are several things a writer can try to ease the manifestations of writer's block in the early stages. In the later stages, when it has become an entrenched psychological problem, nothing short of professional therapy may be of much help, unfortunately.

Many teachers of creative writing are strong advocates of "brainstorming" as a technique for getting their students writing again. Brainstorming will not necessarily cure writer's block, but it is a useful exercise for helping to "unclog" those blocked channels in the brain which inhibit creative flow, and it is very simple to do so. Simply put pen to paper, relax as much as possible and begin to write whatever words flash into your mind. And I mean *whatever* words. If "flibbertigibbet" is the first word that occurs to you, write it down. And then another word, and then another.... The key is to STOP TRYING, to simply let your subconscious take over and see what happens. If *nothing* happens at first, if your mind draws a complete blank, then write down the name of the first thing you look at – your pencil, computer keyboard, a calendar hanging on the wall, a tree visible through an open window – and let these objects lead you to further associations, as far as the trail may lead. And when a phrase, or even a complete sentence, rises out of your subconscious, put that down, too, no matter how absurd or meaningless it sounds. The point is not to write something that you will want to keep, but just to get your writing juices flowing again.

I once had an amazing and totally unexpected success using brainstorming. I hadn't written a word in months; I was deep in the throes of writer's block. One evening, in complete frustration with myself, I sat before my computer keyboard, placed my fingers on the keys and closed my eyes. "You're supposed to be a writer," I told myself in disgust, "so WRITE something." Surrendering totally to whatever gobbledygook my subconscious threw up, I soon found that I had written a sentence that captured my imagination. Where it came from, I have no idea. The line read, *"It had the deepest blue eyes and the curliest dark brown hair."* This seemed to be a description of someone, and, fascinated, I decided to expand on it, letting one thought follow naturally from another. Before the night was over, I had written a short story entitled "The Perfect Robot Baby", which I sold a couple of weeks later to *Woman's Day Magazine* for $1,250.

This is an extreme example of the efficacy of brainstorming, of course. Usually brainstorming is effective only for the very mildest cases of this problem. True writer's block will not succumb so easily, I'm afraid; it requires a more vigorous approach than this type of simple exercise.

So, what do you do when you feel as though you cannot write another word, when you've well and truly "lost it?" There is no simple answer, I fear, but there are things you can try. Unlike many writers and writing instructors, I do not believe that you should force yourself to keep sitting at your keyboard when trying to write has become an agonizing ordeal. What is the point, after all, in trying to force something that simply will not come? When this happens, what you may need is a small vacation from writing, from the self-imposed pressure to keep producing a daily output of words. It is truly a form of torture to sit at the keyboard for hours on end and have nothing to show for it when you are done; it only increases those feelings of inadequacy and failure, and ultimately, despair, that accompany genuine writer's block. This is especially true when writer's block occurs in midst of a project you have been working on for some time; pressuring yourself to keep going at such times will only cause you to lose sight of your original purpose and plan for your story or novel.

What I recommend you do, instead, is put the cover on your keyboard and simply leave it for a few days – in extreme cases, a few weeks, even. Let yourself off the hook, turn to other things, enjoy life and realize that the world will not end if you do not write a certain number of words each day. There are times when we have simply *used up* all our creative energy and are literally running on empty. At such times, a brief respite may help us to "recharge," so that we can eventually return to our work with renewed energy and creativity.

Taking a vacation from writing does not mean that you must stop *learning* about writing, however. This can be the time you use to read the works of the best writers, absorbing and analyzing their styles and techniques, as suggested in the section on *Reading for Technique*. It can also provide an opportunity to explore and research some subject which has always interested you but which you know little about as-yet. In fact, learning about something for the sheer joy of acquiring knowledge and insight is one of the most invigorating and refreshing mental activities you can engage in. And, don't forget, the more you know, the more you will have to write about.

And when you are ready to return to writing, approach it as though you are a patient recovering from a physical illness. Don't be discouraged if you are not able to write at your normal level initially. Test the waters, do only what feels comfortable and no more, and allow yourself to "heal" from the affliction of writer's block at a reasonable pace. If you feel you *must* write something before you are ready to return to your usual routine, try writing character sketches of friends or family members, a detailed description of a real or imagined place, a reminiscence from childhood, *et cetera*. This will help you keep your writing

283

"muscle" in shape without unduly stressing your as-yet fragile psyche.

There are other options you might want to try in dealing with writer's block, as no one method is guaranteed to work with every individual. First of all, you might find it helpful simply to discuss your writer's block with a sympathetic friend or colleague, preferably another writer, who is sure to have a depth of understanding of the problem that a non-writer could not share. But if you are not as-yet acquainted with any other writers, try to find an understanding friend or family member who will be willing to listen, in a sympathetic and non-judgmental way, as you discuss your anxieties about your writing. Often, just expressing a problem to an objective listener gives one a better insight to the problem and its possible solutions. And sometimes others can give us perspectives on our difficulties that we are unable to acquire on our own.

And, finally, there is one other alternative I would like to suggest, one that worked wonders in my own struggle with writer's block, a few years ago. I signed up for a class in English Literature at a local University, hoping only to distract myself temporarily from my despair at being unable to write. What I found, however, was that by the end of the course, I was once again writing freely and with renewed enthusiasm. In fact, so many ideas for writing projects presented themselves to me that I could hardly keep track of them all or bring myself to choose from among them.

How and why did this happen? I believe that it was the impetus I got from being asked to write papers for the class. Writing was no longer an option but an assignment. The instructor of this course demanded that we write daily journal accounts of our impressions of the literary works we were studying, as well as a longer and much more intensely researched term paper. Writing an assignment on a subject not of my choosing seemed to "jog" me out of my writer's block most effectively. In this case, I *had* to write, or fail the course, and my own pride in my intellectual abilities would not allow me to do this. Sometimes, as strange as it may seem, we are able to "rise to the occasion" when given an assignment to write on a specific subject, even when we have felt unable to write on our own.

So, signing up for a course through a community college or an adult education program may prove to be just the therapy you need to help you overcome persistent writer's block. But be sure you choose a subject you find interesting, and make sure it is a course that you know will require a certain amount of writing. Courses in history, literature, psychology, political science or philosophy should meet this requirement.

In the end, however, dealing with and

overcoming writer's block is a very individualized process; what works for one person will not necessarily work for another, and vice versa. But at least now you know some of the methods that have worked for other writers, and I sincerely hope that one of them will work for you.

CONCLUSION

I hope that you have found the discussions in this book helpful to you, in the pursuit of your writing goals. The hard, cold truth is that no one can *teach* you to be a writer, but only a *better* one. If the basic ingredients of raw talent, creative instinct, love of language and the storytelling art are lacking, no teacher on earth can turn you into a successful novelist or short story writer. But for any person who possesses these essential qualities, even those who are already very skilled, there is always something more to learn. In fact, the pursuit of excellence in the craft of writing is a lifelong endeavour, but a most exhilarating one.

As you work to develop your writing skills, I hope that you will always keep in mind that you are not alone in your struggles, though you may often feel that you are. Many, many others share the same drive, the same anxieties, the same pain of rejection, and most of all, the overwhelming impulse toward creative expression.

Good luck! And, *keep writing.*

ABOUT THE AUTHOR

Lynda Fayle Gilmartin is an internationally published author of arresting, original short fiction. A resident of her native Lone Star State, she studied at the University of Texas at Arlington, and earned a Bachelor of Arts degree in English at Texas A&M University-Commerce. Her past work in print news, and magazines, ranges from copy editing to photographic modeling, in addition to authoring several published short stories. This is Ms. Gilmartin's first published collection of original short fiction and nonfiction. She has four adult children.

ABOUT THE ARTIST

Marcelo da Silva Casaquevit is an internationally published illustrator and graphic artist. A native of Brazil, where he lives with his wife, he has depicted vivid, startling imagery for graphic novels, such as *Division Six*, *Grimm Fairy Tales*, and *T.R.A.N.C.E.R.S.* This book marks his first collaboration with Ms. Gilmartin.

www.ingramcontent.com/pod-product-compliance
Lightning Source LLC
Chambersburg PA
CBHW070658180626
46817CB00006B/2422